Storm sat down on her haunches and howled.

"I can't go back! They'll never take me back. And why would I want them to, after what they've done?" she growled to the sky.

But then what would she do? Lone Dog life was too hard, too lonely. She knew that now. Would she just keep walking until she stumbled across a dog Pack who would take her?

No. There's no need. Hope sprang up in Storm's chest. *There are two dogs out there I know would want me in their Pack.*

I just need to find them.

THE GATHERING DARKNESS

THE GATHERING DARKNESS

SURVIVORS

THE EXILE'S JOURNEY

ERIN
HUNTER

HARPER

An Imprint of HarperCollinsPublishers

The Exile's Journey

Copyright © 2018 by Working Partners Limited

Series created by Working Partners Limited

Map art © 2018 by Frank Riccio

Library of Congress Control Number: 2017944389
ISBN 978-0-06-234351-2

Typography based on a design by Hilary Zarycky
18 19 20 21 22 BRR 10 9 8 7 6 5 4 3 2 1
❖
First paperback edition, 2019

Special thanks to Rosie Best

LIGHTHOUSE

UNKNOWN TERRITORY

HIGH WATCH

WILD PACK CA[...]

THE ENDLESS LAKE

LONGPAW TOWN

RIV[...]

FOX DEN

WHISPER'S GRAVE

GIANTFUR CAVE

The Coast

PACK LIST

WILD PACK (IN ORDER OF RANK)

ALPHA:

female swift-dog with short gray fur (also known as Sweet)

BETA:

gold-and-white thick-furred male (also known as Lucky)

HUNTERS:

SNAP—small female with tan-and-white fur

BRUNO—large thick-furred brown male Fight Dog with a hard face

MICKEY—sleek black-and-white male Farm Dog

PATROL DOGS:

MOON—black-and-white female Farm Dog

TWITCH—tan male chase-dog with black patches and three legs

DAISY—small white-furred female with a brown tail

BREEZE—small brown female with large ears and short fur

CHASE—small ginger-furred female

BEETLE—black-and-white shaggy-furred male

THORN—black shaggy-furred female

OMEGA:

small female with long white fur (also known as Sunshine)

PUPS:

FLUFF—shaggy brown female

TUMBLE—golden-furred male

NIBBLE—tan female

TINY—pale-eyed golden female

LONE DOGS:

STORM—brown-and-tan female Fierce Dog

PROLOGUE

Twigs and leaves whipped across Lick's nose as she scrambled through the dark undergrowth. She pinned back her ears and put on a burst of speed. Her belly and chest felt like they were full of stones rattling against her sides, and the pads of her paws were raw and burning from the chase.

Where am I?

Lick stumbled to a halt, pressing her flank to the trunk of a tall tree. She spun around a few times, anxiously flattening the earth, then crouched down between two roots. She made herself as small as she could, tucking her legs underneath her body to stop them from trembling. She could feel her short fur rubbing against the bark. Her shoulder was stiff and sticky with blood, the bites and scratches throbbing with pain.

She panted, searching the air for any scent of Fierce Dogs, but all she could taste was her own panic, foul and bitter.

She could be anywhere. The trees just looked like trees. She might be only a few rabbit-chases from the Wild Pack's territory—or going in completely the wrong direction.

I have to keep running!

But she couldn't get up. She couldn't stop herself from remembering the horrible scene, over and over again:

Her brothers, Wiggle and Grunt, walking just ahead of her. The looming presence of their Fierce Dog Pack surrounding them. The mist closing in, flowing between the trees. The way the Pack had abruptly stopped in the middle of the wood, without any dog making a sound. The cold look in Blade's eyes as she turned and looked at the pups.

The scent of Wiggle's fear.

Blade had smelled it too.

"You are not my pups," Blade had snarled. "You are not my real pups!"

Lick shuddered at the memory and pressed her muzzle into the soft earth, as if the Earth-Dog herself could comfort her.

She and Grunt had both been scared too, but they were better at pretending. Grunt had glowered at Blade, and Lick had watched her intently, waiting to see if this was another test. But

Wiggle had looked up at Blade with soft, wide eyes as dark as his fur. He'd shivered with terror.

And then Blade . . .

Lick wanted to raise her head and howl her grief to the Sky-Dogs, but if the Fierce Dogs found her, she knew, they would kill her.

Just like Blade had killed Wiggle.

The Fierce Dog Alpha's teeth had snapped mercilessly down on the back of Wiggle's neck and she'd shaken him hard, like Lick had seen the Wild Pack do to their prey. When she dropped him, he'd crumpled awkwardly on his side and lay there. Just a few pawsteps from Lick's face. Dead.

"He was no true Fierce Dog," Blade had said. She'd turned her mad eyes and her bloodstained teeth on Lick. Lick had thought her heart would burst out of her chest—then Blade looked at Grunt. "Are you?"

And Grunt . . . Grunt had said, "Yes, I am! I'm a real Fierce Dog! I'll be loyal, I promise. I'll be useful to you!"

"Grunt, no!" Lick had howled, and Blade had turned back to her, teeth scything through the air. Lick had scrambled back as if Lightning had bitten her paws. Blade's fangs had caught and torn the skin on her shoulder, but she'd wriggled out of the Alpha's grip and slipped between Dagger's legs. She'd felt Dagger's body shifting over her head as the big dog tried to turn around in time to catch her. Some dog's claws scraped across her flank, and Lick's fur had rippled with hot breath as another pair of jaws snapped at her and missed.

Blade had howled. The other Fierce Dogs had taken up the howl and huge, heavy pawsteps had thundered after her—but Lick hadn't looked back.

She'd run into the white mist that covered the forest floor, and the wet, cold scent of it had filled her nostrils. It was as if the trees had swallowed her. She'd heard the Fierce Dogs howling behind her in fury and confusion.

Grunt might be a true Fierce Dog, Lick thought, forcing herself to uncurl her paws in the soft earth at the base of the tree. *But I'm not. I'm not like them. I will never, ever be like them.*

She had to find the Wild Pack.

But what if they were sleeping and she led the Fierce Dogs right to them? Would the Fierce Dogs attack? How many dogs might Blade kill, before they could turn and fight?

Lick made herself stand, though her legs wobbled underneath her. She sniffed the air again, trying to block out the acrid smell of her own fear. The forest around her was dark and silent except for the soft rustling of leaves in the wind. All she could scent was mist, mulch, and rot, and the fading trails of small creatures. No Fierce Dogs.

She edged out from the shadow of the tree and began to walk, ignoring the stinging pain in her sides and slipping as quietly as she could between the tangled branches of bushes. Pawstep by pawstep, the farther she walked, the more the crushing terror subsided. Lick began to shiver.

She should never have left the Wild Pack.

What if they wouldn't take her back?

They didn't stop us from leaving, she thought. *Most of them never really wanted us around.*

But Lucky will win them over. He's so good at that. And Martha and Mickey won't let anybody hurt us.

Hurt me.

She'd never been a "me" before. It had always been "us"—she and her litter-brothers stuck together, even when Grunt was being rock-headed and Wiggle was so timid he could barely move. Ever since those days in the Dog-Garden, when they had huddled together underneath the longpaw house, starving and cold, while their Mother-Dog lay dead outside.

Now Grunt had betrayed them, and Wiggle had gone to be

with their Mother-Dog. Lick let out a whine. She hadn't even had a chance to bury him and help him find his way to the Earth-Dog. Would Blade and the Fierce Dogs do it? Lick didn't think so.

She felt as if she'd aged ten moons in one night.

Then suddenly, Lick's nose twitched and her ears pricked up. She scented something familiar—the warm, contented smell of dogs and prey. She opened her mouth to let her tongue loll out, tasting the air until she was certain.

She was going the right way! She'd found the Wild Pack!

Lick broke into another run, this time bounding over the dark mud, hardly feeling the pain in her paws. Yes, there was the strong scent of the Patrol Dogs, a wavering trail outlining the territory. There was Martha's scent, and Lucky's!

She emerged from the line of pine trees into the tall grass, and heard a dog barking—

"It's a pup!"

That was Mickey. Lick put on another burst of speed, scrambling down the slope. Ahead she could make out the dogs—Lucky with his eyes wide and his ears pinned back, the half-wolf Alpha's suspicious glare, Martha's jaws open in surprise and happiness to see her, little Daisy and Sunshine with their tails wagging nervously.

She hurtled toward them, making the last few strides on trembling paws, and let herself stumble and collapse against Mickey's flank.

The other dogs started to ask her questions—What happened? Where were her litter-brothers? How did she get hurt? For a moment, Lick couldn't answer. She just buried her nose in Mickey's side, shuddering and out of breath.

She was safe now. Whatever happened, the Wild Pack was her home now. She would never leave it again.

CHAPTER ONE

I've really messed this up.

Storm's paws skittered across the pale sand, kicking it up behind her as she ran, but she knew she'd never be able to run fast enough.

The big white cliff-bird gave a hoarse shriek, flapped its huge wings, and launched into the air.

It had been sunning itself on a jutting rock in the middle of the beach with its head tucked under its wing: the perfect prey, if Storm had only been patient enough to go around the rock, instead of trying to climb it.

But hunger had made her careless. She'd lost her footing and sent a cluster of pebbles scattering under her paws, and the bird had taken flight.

Instinct told Storm to leap after it, but her weak and tired muscles wouldn't obey her, and she slithered to an undignified stop, her front paws buried in the sand.

She snorted in annoyance at herself as she watched the bird fly off. A good meal, just flapping away into the sky. It was such a waste.

Storm scrabbled out of the sand and shook herself. She trudged on along the edge of the Endless Lake, trying to ignore the rumbling in her belly.

The Sun-Dog's light glinted off the water. It was still and calm today. The sky was clear and cloudless. Storm felt like her fur had only just dried out from the warm rain that had driven all the small prey into their holes and burrows last no-sun, but she could also feel a prickling in her nostrils that told her Lightning and Thunder might be close, and creeping closer on soft paws.

She had to keep going. Perhaps there would be another pool with those little darting brown fish—although they had been barely more than a mouthful for Storm. They were never going to fill her stomach, no matter how easy they were to catch.

Walking on the sand felt harder than it had before. It slipped out from underneath Storm's paws, and she kept losing her balance. She remembered Bella showing her how to keep her tread light so that she wouldn't sink, but she couldn't seem to muster the energy anymore. The skin on her flank and her belly hung loosely.

Would the Pack think I was a big, scary Fierce Dog now? she thought bitterly.

Hunting alone was harder than she'd expected. And, which was almost worse, it was no fun at all. She had only her own eyes to spot prey with, only one nose to scent it with. She didn't have a Scout Dog running ahead to root out the next prey creature. No dog would help her head off a rabbit if it startled, or talk through her tactics with her before she sprang, or reassure her that she would catch something soon when she failed.

She *knew* that Lone Dogs could survive without a Pack, but at the moment she was struggling to see how.

Storm flopped down on the warm sand and let the heavy salt stench of the Endless Lake fill her nostrils.

It smelled of home, but there was something missing. The scents of the Wild Pack.

Several journeys of the Sun-Dog had passed since she had left their camp behind and set out on her own. She had passed the far-thest reach of the Patrol Dogs' scent a long time ago. She'd passed the Light House and shuddered as she remembered poor Spring, washed away when the Wild Pack and the Fierce Dogs had faced off on the narrow hardstone path that led to it.

She was farther from the Pack now than she had ever been before.

I should forget about them. Even if I did want to go back, they wouldn't have me.

In her mind's eye, she could still see them—Alpha and Beta with their pups, Mickey and Snap, Breeze, Chase, Moon and Beetle and Thorn, little Sunshine, and Daisy. . . .

Daisy, who Storm had thought was her friend. But then when it counted, even the small white dog had turned on her.

Storm shook her head and huffed, making tiny specks of sand dance in front of her muzzle. She knew that wasn't fair. She was just grumpy because she was hungry.

Still, it had hurt when Daisy had piped up, *I know something the rest of you don't. Storm walks in her sleep.*

Storm stared out at the Endless Lake, a shiver running through her body, despite the warmth of the Sun-Dog on her flanks. She was remembering. . . .

The Fear-Dog flew before her, huge and terrifying. Gripped in his dark jaws, whimpering and mewling, was a golden pup.

It was Tumble—small, helpless, and vulnerable. And the Fear-Dog was carrying him away.

The memory of the dream still seemed almost as vivid as it had that no-sun. She had been so convinced that the Fear-Dog itself was about to drown Tumble . . . but it had been *her* who had carried the pup to the Endless Lake and left him shivering in a cave, all alone, in the dark. She'd woken up on the beach and run back to the Wild Pack, frantic with worry, not remembering what had happened until Tumble was found and he explained it to his Mother-Dog in a trembling, squeaky voice.

Why did I do it?

Storm knew she might have done the wrong thing, hiding her sleepwalking from them. But she'd done it because she'd known that they would be afraid of her.

And, sure enough, they had been.

None of the Pack trusted her anymore, and how could Storm blame them? She couldn't trust herself. It was better that she'd left. It was better that she was . . . alone.

The Endless Lake gave a soft growl, as if it too was angry with her, and its white, wet paw rose out of the water and crashed on the beach nearby. Storm clambered awkwardly to her paws. The Lake-Dog was right—it wouldn't do any good to lie here and dwell on something she couldn't change.

There was a path close by that led up the cliffs and away from the Endless Lake, through scrubby grass where she thought she might find some small prey, or another chance to catch a cliff-bird. She had to keep trying.

Her paws felt shaky at first on the more solid ground, but soon she was clambering up over the rocks and between tall, spiky bushes with long stems that looked like fuzzy dogs' tails.

She sniffed the ground as she walked, and suddenly, as she reached a single, drooping tree, she smelled something familiar.

That's a dog!

Her ears pricked up, and she took a great sniff of air. A dog had definitely come this way—probably stopped beside this tree, perhaps even slept here. Was it one of the Wild Pack? She couldn't make out the particular scent. And what would they be doing this far from their camp? Maybe it was another dog altogether.

She sniffed harder, but the scent was starting to fade. She could tell now that it was stale. It had been at least a journey of the Sun-Dog since another dog had passed this way. Wishful thinking had made it seem fresher than it was. Storm walked on.

I'm alone. And that's fine.

The Sun-Dog continued on his journey, and still Storm couldn't find any prey she could catch. There had been a rabbit warren, but it was empty. She had given up on trying to catch squirrels before they ran up trees—her limbs felt weak and clumsy, and she couldn't leap or balance on her thin back legs.

She moved away from the Endless Lake, turning inland but always keeping the scent of the lake on her left, so she could be sure she was moving farther and farther from the Wild Pack. She walked through a thick wood of pine trees, the needles bursting with scent as she trod over them. Then she climbed up a rocky slope and found herself looking down the other side at the steep, muddy bank of a river.

It was much less full than the river that she knew—the one where she had finally beaten Blade on the ice, and where she and Lucky had taught the pups that they didn't need to be afraid of the River-Dog. This was like the smaller littermate of that river, a wide muddy basin with only a trickling stream winding between the rocks and a few sprouting green stalks.

Did the River-Dog not like this place? Was her attention turned elsewhere? Or was this the very end of the other river's tail? Did it run in a big loop around the Pack's territory?

Across the stream, Storm looked up and saw more pine trees, rising toward something strange in the distance. It took her a long moment of staring to realize that it was like a hill—but taller than any she had ever seen before. It rose up and up and up into the sky, so big it vanished into the clouds and she couldn't even see the top.

Could a dog walk that far? Could they live in the sky, near the clouds?

Storm shook herself—she would never make it that far if she didn't find something to eat. Still, she couldn't help feeling a stir of adventure in her heart. A dog without a Pack could go wherever she wanted, couldn't she?

I wonder what Lucky would say if he saw this. . . .

For now, she decided to follow the stream. Perhaps she could catch something on the edge of the water. If she walked in the mud, the prey wouldn't catch her scent.

She had gone a few rabbit-chases when, sure enough, a bird landed on a rock sticking out in the middle of the stream. It was really big, even fatter than the cliff-bird, with black feathers that glistened as a few drops of rain began to fall.

More rain, Storm sighed. She would have found somewhere to shelter—but the bird was paying her no attention, searching in the mud of the river bottom, probably looking for worms.

Storm crept closer, ignoring the rain, keeping her head low to the ground, moving as slowly as she dared. She was glad she was downwind, even though birds didn't seem to scent things the way dogs did.

The drops of rain were growing heavier and closer together, splashing in the mud at her paws and beating across her back. She blinked water out of her eyes, focused only on her prey. The rain was good—it would muffle the sound of her approach, as well as her scent. The mud was growing stickier and slipperier, but she kept her footing, even though she knew she would have to spend a long time later getting the earth out from between her toes.

The bird was hunched now, its feathers ruffled up around its neck, as if it was making the same decision as Storm—*shelter, or food?* Storm was a few pawsteps from being close enough to pounce when its neck suddenly rose and its beak twisted around, sending raindrops spinning off into the air. But it wasn't looking at Storm—it was looking farther upstream, toward something Storm couldn't see. It took flight with another arcing spray of water and vanished into the trees.

"*Sky-Dogs!*" Storm growled. "Can't I have one piece of good—"

She broke off. Something was happening. The mud around her paws was washing away. The stream had grown wider and deeper, surrounding Storm and covering most of the muddy basin. Even as she stood still, the water buffeted at the ground underneath her, and she struggled to keep her balance. Then there was a wet crashing sound, and up ahead, a wall of water sloshed around the corner of a rock, right toward Storm.

River-Dog! Help me! Storm thought, trying to turn and scramble for the bank, but the stream underpaw was a river now, and she splashed and slipped as she turned. The wave hit her while she was off-balance, knocking her off her paws. She rolled over and spun around, trying to reach for something solid to hold on to, but there was nothing but mud and water. The river closed over her head. Freezing panic seized her throat, and she paddled as hard as she could against the River-Dog's current, breaking the surface just long enough to feel the air and rain on her muzzle before she was pushed under again.

This was worse than splashing in the Endless Lake, with its constant push and pull, and much worse than the steady river she knew—the River-Dog was running as if she was being chased by something!

Storm kicked out and broke through the surface again, just in time for another wave to crash over her, blinding her for a moment. There were no scents except for mud and panic.

You're a big, strong Fierce Dog, she thought. *It's just water!*

But the water was so big, and Storm felt very small, as if she was still a pup and she would be swept away if Martha didn't come to her rescue any moment.

In fact, through the splashing waves and the pounding rain, she thought could almost see the enormous water-dog, her giant black paws striking the surface as she swam with the current toward Storm.

She was so swift and graceful in the water. . . .

Storm couldn't breathe without sucking in water, and the cold was making her legs ache as she scrambled for a hold on the mud, but she thought she saw Martha moving toward her, and a small voice in her mind said, *It'll be all right, Martha will save us.* Her panic subsided.

But then the shape reached Storm and passed.

Martha, wait! Storm twisted to follow the dark dog-shape. Martha was leaving her behind! Storm tossed her head back and tried to copy Martha's swimming movements, just as she and Grunt and Wiggle had done as pups, just as she'd taught Lucky and Sweet's pups to do.

As she swam, the dark shape became less like a dog and more like a wave. It rolled and vanished into the water. Storm swam on, exhausted and grateful to Martha—or had it been the River-Dog?

Perhaps it was both. Between them, they had sent her a memory.

Sometimes, the worst thing you can do is fight the current, Martha had said. *A dog can never win that fight.*

And sure enough, it was easier to stay above the water now that she was facing the same direction as the wave and not trying to fight it. She could even push herself off small rocks and move, bit by bit, over toward the bank.

Finally, the mud beneath her was solid enough for her to dig in her claws, and she half-dragged herself and half-ran out of the water and up onto solid, sticky ground. She stumbled and crawled along the bank until she was away from the river, on ground that was thick with grass and thin, creaking saplings.

She flopped down, her flanks heaving.

Martha, thank you.

The breath rasped in Storm's throat and the rain beat down on her, but she didn't mind. It was washing some of the mud from her fur, and when she caught a little on her tongue, it tasted fresh and clean.

Just stop fighting. Turn and ride the current, she thought. *Oh, Martha. Perhaps if I'd listened to you, I would have left the Wild Pack long ago. . . .*

Fighting her Packmates' fears had been like trying to swim

upstream into a rushing tide. It was a fight that Storm was never going to win. The knowledge was uncomfortable, like lying here in the grass in the rain, but if she hadn't made that decision, their terror would have drowned her.

CHAPTER TWO

Storm paused in the shade of a pine tree to shake out her fur yet again. Drops spattered the tree trunks and splashed in the undergrowth. She should be dry by now, but it seemed as if between the rain and the river she had been soaked all the way down to her bones.

She wasn't quite sure where she was. She was in new territory, of course, but before the river she had at least had an idea in her head of how far she was from the Pack and from the Endless Lake, and which direction she was heading in. She wished she could catch another glimpse of that hill in the clouds, so she would know which way she was facing—but the trees were too thick, and the forest floor sloped steeply up and down all the time. Even the Sun-Dog was no help, hiding behind the clouds and casting a vague, pale light that didn't throw proper shadows.

Why does it matter? she wondered. *Do you think you'll need to find your way back one day? Why try to keep track—wherever you are, there's your Pack, right?*

Storm growled at herself. There was no point feeling sad about being *lost*, even if her paws were constantly sticky with mud, even if her fur was wet and hanging loose and she was *so hungry*. . . .

It didn't matter where she was, because she had no home, and no dog would care enough to find her.

That was a very dark thought, and Storm tried to shake it off and keep her tail high as she moved through the forest, sniffing the ground and the trees for signs of prey.

She caught a familiar scent she couldn't quite place—was it a dog, or prey, or neither? She decided to follow it, glad to have an aim for now, even if it didn't lead her directly to her next meal.

As she walked, she couldn't seem to stop thinking about the Wild Pack.

Their first Alpha had never liked Storm. The half wolf, half dog had refused to let her have her Naming Ceremony, or to call her by her name when she chose it. When Storm thought about how she'd had to fight to be who she was—*Storm*, and not *Savage*—her fur prickled and a growl rumbled in her throat.

Then she hushed. Her nose twitched.

There was prey nearby! It was a rabbit, and it had passed this way very recently, after the rainfall. It smelled delicious. Storm could feel her mouth watering and opened her jaws to taste the air, working out which way the rabbit had passed. She followed carefully, determined not to lose her prey this time.

But the old Alpha's face kept swimming to the front of her thoughts, even though she knew she should be focusing on the hunt.

Of course, the old Alpha hadn't remained Alpha. He had allied himself with the Fierce Dogs in the end. Storm couldn't understand it. He had hated them so much, he had driven Grunt to leave the Wild Pack and become Fang, a true Fierce Dog. And yet, the Alpha had joined them too. He'd been their Omega.

She remembered his cruel yellow eyes, the way he used to stare at the Fierce pups as if they had personally offended him. The other dogs in the Wild Pack were afraid of Fierce Dogs after their encounters at the Dog-Garden, but she'd always had the sense that the half wolf's dislike ran deeper than that, somehow.

What did Fierce Dogs ever do to you? she wondered. *And why can't I clear you out of my mind now?*

A few cautious pawsteps later, Storm peered around a tall pine tree and saw that she'd come to a small clearing. The ground was grassier and uneven with dug earth, and right there, nibbling on a dandelion leaf, was the rabbit. It looked a bit skinny, but it would be enough to give Storm some of her strength back. And she wouldn't have to share it with any other dog, either.

But rabbits were fast. Storm tried to ignore the drool that dripped from her teeth as she sniffed at the creature's scent. She had to be careful and smart about this, or her prey would definitely get away—some rabbits could run so fast they even outpaced Sweet, and she was a swift-dog.

Storm stepped quietly, thankful now for the mud on her paws and on the ground that muffled her movements, until she was behind a large boulder, keeping the rabbit firmly upwind. She wished she could make a leap for it—all this sneaking around was more like *sharpclaw* behavior, not how a dog should hunt. But if she did, there'd be no dog to flank the rabbit and take it down. Storm could eat, or not, and it was all up to her.

The rabbit turned to pick another dandelion leaf, hopping so that its back was turned on Storm.

She wasn't going to get a better chance. Trying not to so much as breathe, she crept out from behind the boulder and picked her way, paw by paw, across the clearing.

Then suddenly, a puff of air crossed the back of Storm's head, stirring the drying fur behind her ears. The wind was changing direction.

Now it was Storm who was upwind of the rabbit, and her scent that was being carried across the clearing.

No! Wind-Dogs, what are you doing?

The rabbit's ears went up and its nose twitched. Its black eye blinked, and then it was gone in a scramble, kicking up pine needles behind it.

"No!" Storm barked aloud. Her back legs kicked out and she sprang after the rabbit, forcing her tired limbs into a galloping sprint. The pale gray shape skidded around a tree and through a bush, and Storm crashed after it. It was futile, Storm knew deep down. The creature was faster than her, especially in the forest, but she was desperate. She had to try.

Bounding over branches and under bushes, Storm kept the rabbit in sight, a gray blur of panic, until she reached the edge of the trees. If she was lucky, the rabbit would try to go to ground and she could dig it out—

But as they burst from the trees onto a scrubby slope, the wind kicked up once again and threw a flurry of leaves and pine needles across Storm's vision. She squeezed her eyes closed to protect them, and her paws came down unevenly on the side of the hill. She stumbled and skidded, digging in her claws to stop herself from tumbling down the slope.

I've lost it, she thought, her eyes still closed, shaking her head frantically to try and clear the leaves and dust that had been blown into her face.

But then she heard a sound—a thumping of large paws, a growl, and a wet snap.

Something else was on the slope with her. Something like a dog—but not a dog.

She opened her eyes gingerly and looked across the brush.

It was a wolf.

The creature was larger than Storm, with thick gray fur and yellow eyes. It had the rabbit's body hanging limply in its jaws. As she watched, the wolf met her eyes and dropped the prey between its big paws.

That's the scent I picked up earlier, Storm thought, her heart in her mouth. *That's why I was thinking about our old Alpha!*

Oh, Sky-Dogs—am I on wolf territory?

CHAPTER THREE

Storm turned on the spot to face the wolf, trying to keep her footing on the steep slope, sending more pine needles skidding away down the hill. She tensed, ready to spring if she had to.

I need that meal more than you do. I may be weak, but I'm desperate, and I'll show you how a desperate Fierce Dog can fight. . . .

The wolf sniffed the air as if trying to get the measure of Storm. She shuddered as she gazed into his yellow eyes, so like the Wild Pack's former Alpha.

The half-wolf was the first dog in the Pack that wouldn't accept us Fierce pups. If he had been kind, would the others have followed his example?

But this wasn't Alpha. The wolf didn't pick up the rabbit and run off, or growl and crouch to spring in an attack. He tilted his head and watched Storm with interest, but no fear.

"Good teamwork, dog," he said.

Storm was stunned into silence for a long moment. "I was hunting alone," she growled back at last.

The wolf opened his jaws and panted. "Oh, then should I have let it go? If I hadn't leaped in when I did, this rabbit would be halfway to the Great Water by now."

Great Water? thought Storm. *Could that be a wolf's name for the Endless Lake?*

"In fact," the wolf continued, "it was moving so fast when I caught it, I think I might have loosened a tooth."

He stepped over the prey and advanced toward Storm. Storm had to dig her claws into the soft ground to stop herself from backing off.

He opened his jaws and ran his large red tongue over his fangs experimentally.

"What do you think? Anything knocked loose?"

"What?" Storm snarled. "No, they look fine."

"Well, that's good. Wily once knocked out one of his teeth, and he didn't stop complaining about the pain for many moons."

The wolf turned away. Storm watched him carefully. Was all this some sort of trick? He was behaving as if he trusted her, a strange dog whose prey he had . . . well, perhaps not *stolen*, but certainly *got*. Was he expecting her to leap for the rabbit while his back was turned? Or try to attack him? If she wanted to get it away from him, she was going to need to be sneaky. She wasn't ready for a fight. . . .

But then the wolf nudged the rabbit with his nose and turned back to Storm.

"Shall we share, since we caught the prey together?"

Really? Storm thought. The wolf was waiting for her to respond, his teeth close to the prey but not tearing into it yet. She sniffed the air, but apart from the strong scent of pine and this wolf, she couldn't smell much else.

Cautiously, she padded over to the wolf. He pressed one paw against the rabbit and tore loose a mouthful of flesh, swallowing it down with a happy gulp. Storm leaned in and did the same, relishing the warm, fresh meat. She hadn't had a proper meal in days and hadn't had rabbit since she left the Wild Pack. It took only a few delicious mouthfuls for her to start to feel stronger again.

It was strange, sharing prey like this—one mouthful at a time, instead of taking her turn at the prey pile and eating until she'd had her fill. Was this how wolves always ate? Wouldn't this wolf be in trouble for eating before his Pack?

She was starting to realize that all she knew about wolves was connected to the Wild Pack's old Alpha—and this wolf was nothing like him.

"Do you have a name?" she asked, through a mouthful of rabbit.

"Thoughtful," said the wolf. Storm looked at him, tilting her head to one side.

"That's a strange name."

"Not for a wolf," said Thoughtful blandly. "Several of my ancestors have had the same name. What should I call you?"

"Storm," said Storm. Thoughtful huffed through his teeth.

"Now that *is* a strange name! Why did your Pack call you that?"

Storm frowned, but her ears twitched with amusement. "I chose it myself. That's what dogs do, when they're old enough to lose their pup name. Do wolf Packs choose names for each other?"

"Of course. We are named for our natures, and who knows you better than your Pack? Why did you pick the name Storm?"

Storm had just taken a big mouthful of rabbit, and she chewed it slowly, pretending that she couldn't speak because she was too busy eating.

Why did I? It felt right. Lucky talked so much about the Storm of Dogs . . .

perhaps it was my destiny, to kill Blade and stop her prophecy coming true?

Or perhaps it was something else. My presence in the Pack has always been stormy. Is Storm a name that fits me like Thoughtful fits this wolf? Would the Wild Pack say so?

Am I a storm that blew through the Pack and almost destroyed it?

"You aren't used to being so hungry," Thoughtful said, snapping Storm out of her thoughts, and she looked up guiltily. She'd been eating the rabbit, lost in thought—she knew she'd had several mouthfuls more than her fair share. Thoughtful sat back on his haunches and licked his lips, as if he had already eaten his fill. Storm was too hungry to be polite—if he didn't want the rabbit, she did.

"I'm not," she said through another mouthful, answering the question Thoughtful hadn't quite asked. "I don't like it much either."

"I thought not. You have the frame of a dog who's used to being well fed. You grew up in a good Pack." His ears sagged back against his head in genuine sadness, and he said quietly, "Did something terrible happen?"

Yes. Several terrible things. But I don't think that's what you mean.

"The Pack is fine. I left them. I'm a Lone Dog now. And I don't really want to talk about it," she added, trying to head off the questions she could see forming behind Thoughtful's eyes. He nodded, but she could tell he was still turning the idea over in his mind. He really *had* been named well—he couldn't seem to *stop* thinking.

"Are dogs very casual creatures?" he asked eventually. "I can't imagine any wolf leaving their Pack just like that. Do dog Packs break up often?" He gave an amused snort. "I suppose there are no dogs called Faithful or Loyal. . . ."

Storm's fur bristled.

"We don't wear our traits as names, but that doesn't mean we don't have them," she snapped. "You'd know that if you met the Pack. There are plenty of faithful *and* loyal dogs. It's a lot more complicated than that."

"Are you looking for a Pack? For other dogs?"

"No." To Storm's own surprise, that answer came easily. She raised her head and tried to look as firm as she could. That was the decision she had made, the one that made sense for all dogs.

If only it didn't sting so much.

She forced herself to keep her head high.

Thoughtful gazed back and nodded. "It seems a shame for you to be a—what did you call it? A Lone Dog? If you were stronger, you'd be an asset to any Pack. And you didn't attack me, even though you thought I'd stolen your prey," he added, with a glint of humor in his yellow eyes. He paused, as if he was expecting Storm to reply. But Storm didn't quite know what to say.

Thank you? I'm glad you think I'm a good dog? Or do you want me to tell you all about why I left? Thoughtful was going to be disappointed if that was true—Storm wasn't sure she *could* explain everything that had happened with the traitor, the Fear-Dog, the pups, Whisper's and Bruno's deaths, the foxes, the longpaws. . . .

Thoughtful lay down on his side and rolled in the pine needles.

"It's good if you've got an itch," he explained, when he saw Storm tilting her head at him in puzzlement. "And it helps with hunting around here if you smell like the forest. You still smell like you've come from far away, near the Great Water. It'll be easier to catch prey if you have the right scent."

Storm hesitated, but what did she have to lose? She lay down and rolled over a few times in the crunchy, fragrant needles. Thoughtful was right; it did feel good on her back.

"What about your Pack? Will you get in trouble, if they find out you shared this prey with me?" Storm asked. The wolf could answer one of her questions, for a change. "We used to get away with eating on a hunt, if we were very hungry, but Alpha would be cross if we didn't bring anything back."

"It's the same with wolves," Thoughtful said, still upside down with his belly exposed to the sky, as if he didn't have a worry in the world. "The Pack won't be impressed if I come back with rabbit between my teeth and none for the prey store."

"Don't you hunt together?" Storm said, lying down and holding the remains of the rabbit between her paws, determined to get every bite out of the prey that she could.

"Sometimes," Thoughtful said. "But I don't like to hunt in a Pack. Too noisy, too rowdy. A Pack of wolves can bring down any prey they like," he added, with a note of pride in his voice, "but I prefer to hunt alone. Gives me time to think."

"Of course it does," Storm muttered into the bones of the rabbit. "So why *did* you share the prey with me? You didn't have to."

Thoughtful turned his yellow eyes on her and rolled to his feet, shaking out his shaggy gray fur and showering pine needles on the ground.

"You looked hungry," he said simply.

How many dogs would do the same? Storm wondered. *Especially for a not-dog? Would I have done it for him?*

"Do dog Packs have a lot of rules?" Thoughtful asked, scratching behind his ear.

"*Lots*," said Storm emphatically. "But they can change from one journey of the Sun-Dog to the next. It all depends on what the Pack needs—and how the Alpha wants to run things."

"What's a Sun-Dog?" Thoughtful asked, and Storm stared at him.

"What's *the* Sun-Dog?" she echoed. She looked up. The Sun-Dog was there, more than halfway through his journey from one horizon to the other, traveling down the sky toward his den. "That is! The Spirit Dog that shines light down from the sky. There!"

She gestured with her nose, and Thoughtful looked up. His ears twitched with amusement.

"That looks like a dog to you? How silly!"

"Well, *no*," Storm said. "Spirit Dogs don't *look* like dogs—but they still *are* dogs. And he's so far away and so bright, how can you know what he really looks like?"

"Spirit Dogs, huh?" Thoughtful stared up at the Sun-Dog for a moment longer and then looked away, blinking. "You have a point. After all, we don't *see* the Great Wolf, or the ancestors who go to her caverns when they die, but we know she lives on the moon. I suppose that's no stranger than thinking the sun is really a dog."

She lives on *the Moon-Dog?* Storm thought. The idea twisted her brain in a strange way. Did that mean that the dead wolves and their Great Wolf were like tiny fleas living on the Moon-Dog's back? Or could the Moon-Dog and the Great Wolf actually be the same thing? After all, the Moon-Dog was silver, like a wolf. . . .

Storm blinked the thoughts aside. She wasn't sure she liked the idea of being watched over by a wolf at night.

"Well, I would like to hear more of your dog stories sometime, but for now I must go." Thoughtful stretched hugely, pushing his forepaws out in front of him and wagging his tail in the air. "Storm, Lone Dog, thank you for your company and allowing me to share your meal. I wish you luck on your travels. A word of advice, though—if you're going to linger near here, you should be careful not to stray onto my Pack's territory. Wolves don't like other hunters to pass the Dead Tree."

Storm cocked her head nervously. "I don't know where that is."

"You'll know it if you see it," said Thoughtful. "It's a few rabbit-chases from here. It's very large and very dead. Stay this side of it and you'll be all right."

Storm knew that this was a reasonable request—after all, dogs wouldn't want wolves wandering onto their territory either.

"Not all wolves are as friendly as I am. Especially in large numbers," Thoughtful said, turning to go. "Be careful, Storm."

I'm sure they're not, Storm thought. "I was lucky to run into you," she said out loud. "Good luck on your hunt, Thoughtful the Wolf. I'll share prey with you anytime!"

Thoughtful let out a woof of amusement and trotted away, his tail wagging.

After he had gone, Storm stretched out too, finally feeling strong enough to try hunting again. This time she would catch something all by herself. She was a Lone Dog now, and she was going to act like it.

Still, as she looked around, down the steep scrubby slope to another dark patch of forest and up toward the faint gray outline of the land in the clouds, she wished that Thoughtful didn't have to leave.

There was plenty to explore, in this strange land of kind wolves—but, like her whole future, she was going to have to explore it all alone.

CHAPTER FOUR

The last few journeys of the Sun-Dog had been better for Storm. She had caught more prey, taking Thoughtful's advice about hiding her scent and learning to move more quietly along the crunchy, crackly forest floor. She was getting stronger, and she felt as dry and warm as she had before she'd fallen in the river.

But there was still a feeling in her belly, almost as uncomfortable as the pangs of hunger. It felt as if she had gotten tangled in a thick vine and it was tugging at her.

It wanted her to turn back.

Though she hadn't strayed too far from where she'd met the wolf, she was still farther than ever from the Wild Pack camp. And in six—or was it seven?—Sun-Dog journeys, she hadn't spoken to another creature apart from Thoughtful.

And now, an instinct she didn't even know she had was pulling at her, whispering in her ears: *It's not safe to be out here alone. It's not right to be alone. Turn back, before it's too late.*

But it was already too late. Storm had been trying to ignore the urge for a while now, but the thin voice wouldn't be quiet, and it wouldn't listen to reason, no matter how many times she told herself that going back was impossible, that she would still be alone even if she was closer to the Wild Pack. Sweet and Lucky wouldn't let her come back, even if they wanted her to—there were too many dogs who were afraid of her.

She would never see either of them again, nor their pups. Storm tried not to think about Nibble, Tumble, Fluff, and little Tiny. Whenever she did, the dream of the Fear-Dog seemed to rise up like a shadow and cast her mind into darkness. Her ears felt as heavy as rocks, and she walked with her head hanging low.

The bad dog is still there, you know it is. What if you've left the pups in danger . . .

"But they wouldn't take me back," she growled out loud, startling a small bird that perched halfway up the tree she was passing by. "There's nothing I can do! Anyway, Lucky and Sweet aren't stupid, even if they are a bit . . . well, they won't let anything happen to their pups, and neither will the other good dogs."

The silence of the forest felt strangely judgmental, as if all the birds and prey animals were thinking, *Won't they? Are you sure?*

Storm shook her head.

I need to keep moving forward. She knew if she let herself get sad, or worry too much about the bad dog, she wouldn't have the energy to hunt. The days before Thoughtful's intervention had been terrible. She never wanted to feel that hungry and weak again.

I'm a one-dog Pack now. I've got to look after myself first.

And that meant knowing everything there was to know about the place she was living—including all about her potential enemies. She stopped and sniffed around a thornbush, and found a clump of gray hair caught on one of the stems.

The wolf Pack's camp must be nearby.

As she had been making her den the previous night, curling up in the shelter of an overhanging rock, she had smelled them. Not just Thoughtful, but at least four different wolf scents, being carried on the wind from somewhere not too far away.

She had decided then that as soon as the Sun-Dog woke her up, she would go out and scout their camp.

I know Thoughtful warned me, but . . . I need to know just where this Dead Tree is, at least. She thought, *I don't know if a wolf's "rabbit-chase" is the same distance as ours!* And yes, perhaps she was lonely. The idea of spending more time with the wolves, even just watching from a distance, stopped her from feeling pulled back toward the Wild Pack. It was like finding just the right tree trunk to scratch an itch you couldn't reach.

In any case, she was curious too. She wanted to see how wolves organized their Packs, and how they dealt with one another. Would it be very different from the dogs she'd known?

Thoughtful had been right: she did know the Dead Tree when she saw it. It was tall, almost as tall as the healthy trees around it, but its surface was black and flaking away, and the ground all around it smelled strongly of ash.

Beyond it, there was another rocky slope. Storm was growing used to the way the land here rose and fell in peaks and valleys, as if some enormous dog had clawed deep furrows out of the ground. But this one was different. As Storm crept past the Dead Tree, she saw that the sides of the valley were vertical, flat, gray, and regular-looking. It was strange—the last time she had seen edges like that on stone, it had been in the longpaw place where they were putting up their new dens. But if longpaws had ever been here, they definitely weren't now—lush green grasses and bushes sprang up between the strange straight cracks in the valley walls, and at the bottom there was a small lake. A well-trodden path wound down between the steep drops toward the edge of the lake, and beside the water there was a group of gray wolves, lying in the sun. Their camp must be down there, among the greenery, near the water.

Well, Storm thought, *I may be a little past the tree, but unless those wolves have wings, I am certainly not within three or even four rabbit-chases.*

Satisfied with her logic, she lay down on a flat block of stone to watch the camp.

There were several paths down into the valley, one directly opposite her and one somewhere to her right. She spotted a group of wolves emerging from the undergrowth on the other side of the valley and lay as still as she could, knowing she was exposed, but if she didn't move, they probably wouldn't see her.

Luckily for her, the wolves were occupied—they were dragging prey with them, taking it in turns to clamp their strong jaws around the antlers or spindly legs of something as big as two of them put together. It flashed lightly gold in the bright sunlight.

Storm's heart gave a little jolt. *A deer!* It was enormous. What would happen if some wolf took down the Golden Deer? Would they even know about the blessing of the Wind-Dogs? Sweet had said that the Golden Deer would bring good fortune to any Pack that caught it. Storm and Lucky had been determined to bring it back for their pups, and for the Wild Pack. But when she'd seen it in the distance, on her long walk out of the Wild Pack's territory, Storm had decided to let it go.

Is it my fault if the wolf Pack caught it instead?

But she realized quickly that the creature was just a very large ordinary stag, paler in color than the bright creature she'd caught glimpses of.

They dragged, pushed, and even head-butted the creature down the slope to their camp, the sound of their barks and growls reaching Storm even though she couldn't make out the words. They worked together as a team, each taking their turn to pull, and using their break time to sit back and watch and warn the others if there was a big rock or a drop ahead.

Storm sighed. She missed being part of a hunting party. When it was going well, it was wonderful, working so closely with other dogs who all had the same aim.

This deer would easily have fed the Wild Pack for two whole journeys of the Sun-Dog. Did the wolf Pack always eat this well, or would these wolves be greeted like heroes?

Looking around, Storm decided that if there were patrol wolves, then they were obviously elsewhere right now. It couldn't hurt just to creep a little bit closer—there was a spot farther down the path that overlooked the camp and was furnished with green shrubs that would do perfectly to hide Storm while she watched the wolves.

I'll be gone before they have any idea I was here, she thought, placing her paws carefully on the loose stones of the path and creeping closer.

The hunters reached the camp while Storm was moving into her new position. When she was settled and she looked down again, the wolves had gathered by the side of the lake. They formed a wide circle. Storm counted thirteen wolves. Thoughtful was there, speaking with a female wolf who sat beside him, but Storm couldn't hear what he was saying.

One very large wolf stepped forward, raised her muzzle, and howled. It was a sound that thrilled and frightened Storm all at once. This had to be the Alpha. Storm could just about make out a large bald patch on her front leg, probably a scar from some wolf battle. Part of Storm longed to hear the story of it, but the more sensible parts of her were glad that she would probably never get close enough to do that.

"Great Wolf," the Alpha howled. "We thank you for the good hunting, and we thank the hunters who have brought us this feast."

One by one, the wolves all howled more quietly, echoing the words of their Alpha—"Great Wolf, we thank you!"

Then all the wolves advanced on the deer. All of them at once! Storm stared, trying to make out Thoughtful in the crowd of gray fur and wagging tails that surrounded the deer carcass. They didn't wait their turn—they shared, just like Thoughtful had done, all of them together. Even the Alpha had to tear off strips of prey alongside her wolves. But Storm supposed that when there was always plenty to go around, it wasn't so important to make sure the leaders and hunters ate first.

There was only one wolf who hadn't joined in on the feeding frenzy. He was thin and his coat was slightly matted. For a moment, Storm wondered if this was their Omega, being forced to wait until the end. But then she saw Thoughtful and the she-wolf he'd been talking to before peel away from the deer, chunks of prey held in their mouths. They brought them to the wolf and laid them at his paws with obvious reverence. When the wolf bent down to pick them up, Storm realized that he was just old— perhaps very old. He trembled when he moved, and the female paused, pushing the meat in front of his nose, as if she wanted to make sure he could scent where his meal was after the first bite. Was he blind? Or just very frail? Storm almost felt she could hear his bones creaking.

It all felt very strange to her, the Alpha eating with everybody else, and only one elderly wolf keeping himself separate. But then, what would wolves think of the dog way of doing things, with a Pack's strict rules about eating in turn?

Storm's stomach growled. All of this thinking about food was making her hungry, and there was a tasty scent somewhere nearby. It was probably squirrel—there were lots of the little fast creatures around here, probably quite safe from the wolves, who clearly focused on much bigger prey.

But not me, she thought, turning and stalking toward the trees, sniffing carefully. *I'm a Lone Dog, and I'll eat you up. . . .*

Sure enough, about a dog-length up the trunk of a tree, a gray and fuzzy shape hung upside down with its claws. Storm crouched behind another tree, watching, uncertain whether it was going up or coming down. She would have liked to be able to walk up trees as easily as she could run across the ground.

She was in luck. The squirrel ran down the tree and paused, digging at the ground, upwind of where Storm was crouched. She sprang, meeting her prey jaws-first. That was one thing she had learned from hunting alone—when you had only one chance to catch your dinner, you had to make each bite count.

She was about to devour the prey where she sat, but then she looked behind her. She could still hear the odd growl or bark from the wolves' camp, and she was still on the valley side of the Dead Tree. *Technically*, this squirrel had been hunted on their territory, and if they found its bones chewed up there, they would probably have some questions. So she picked up the limp carcass in her jaws and trotted away to the place she had made her den, where she could finish her meal without being interrupted.

Being a Lone Dog is almost like being a wolf, she thought. *I don't have to wait for anyone!* But it wasn't, really. She didn't have other dogs snuffling beside her, sharing her space and her prey. And she hadn't called out to the Great Wolf to thank her for the hunt, either.

"Thank you, Forest-Dog," she muttered, through a mouthful of food. "For this tasty squirrel, and for not letting me starve even though I tried quite hard. . . ."

It wasn't a very funny joke, but that was fine, because there was no dog there to laugh at it either way. Sunshine would have laughed. So would Whisper. Lucky and Twitch would both have shaken their heads and rolled their eyes.

Thoughts of the Wild Pack were like predators, following her—hunting her, wherever she went. Lurking in the shadows until it was time to strike, and easily able to take her down.

She imagined them stepping up to eat—Sweet first, and then the pups and Lucky. Twitch, Mickey, Snap, Daisy, Breeze . . . they paraded in front of her mind's eye. But it wasn't a soothing memory. As each dog passed before Storm, she had to wonder . . .

Are you the bad dog? Twitch, Snap, Chase? Mickey, Sunshine?

Have you been killing your Packmates?

And have you stopped now that I've left you alone—or are they all still in terrible danger?

Storm jerked awake into darkness. For a moment, she didn't know where she was—she was lying in an unfamiliar place, surrounded by the smells of the forest, and there was no sign of the other hunters who should be in the den with her, no scent and no warmth coming from their sleeping bodies.

Then she remembered that she was alone in her new den, under the hanging rock, just as she heard another plaintive howl cut through the quiet night air.

The wolves! Something's happening!

She had been back to the valley a few times now. However much she watched them, it never seemed to sate her curiosity completely. She would be hunting some prey in the part of the forest she thought of as "hers," when suddenly she would be overcome with the desire to know what was happening down in the wolf camp. She just liked to watch them go about their tasks as a

Pack, working together, playing, sometimes arguing. Their huge Alpha would settle disputes quickly—no wolf wanted to be on the receiving end of those enormous jaws—and everything would settle back to a peaceful, ordinary existence. It was so unlike the Wild Pack way of doing things . . . and so much like it, at the same time.

They had never howled in the middle of the night before.

She padded through the dark undergrowth and past the Dead Tree, until she came to her favorite vantage point. When she looked down, her breath caught in her chest.

The wolf Pack was on the move. All of them, from the youngest, still barely out of puphood with oversized paws and huge dark eyes, to the very old wolf she had seen Thoughtful and his friend feeding several times. They walked slowly, not at all like a hunt setting out. Storm followed them, staying carefully downwind and up on the lip of the valley, while the Pack moved in a slow procession away from the lake and toward the wider, shallower end of the valley.

The wild bushes and trees gave way to a wide grassy plain, and Storm's path along the top sloped sharply down to meet it. She moved more carefully, aware that soon she would lose the safety of the cliff and be truly trespassing on the wolves' territory. The plain was silvery in the strong light of the Moon-Dog, and in the middle of it, a large slab of white stone stood all by itself. The wolves, who had been marching slowly but unstoppably, suddenly paused. They seemed reluctant to approach the white stone at first, spreading out into a circle around it. Then one wolf stepped forward—the elderly wolf Storm had seen before, walking at the head of the Pack with the Alpha by his side.

His limbs trembled as, with some difficulty, he clambered up onto the white stone and flopped down with his muzzle on his forepaws.

The Wolf Alpha also stepped forward, but she didn't go too near the stone. Instead she turned and faced the circle of wolves with another piercing, melancholy howl.

"Great Wolf, the time has come for our Packmate to return to you. He brings his loyalty, his honor, and the boundless love of his pups and of their pups. Please, welcome him home to the caverns of the moon, where he will forever be with the wolves of the past."

Storm's breath caught in her throat, a great wave of sadness making her choke.

The elderly wolf was dying. That was what Thoughtful had told her, wasn't it—that dead wolves went to the moon to be with the Great Wolf and their ancestors?

In turn, more wolves stepped forward and howled—they howled to the Great Wolf, and to the elderly wolf on the white stone, and to one another. One told a story about the elderly wolf bringing down a bear all by himself, and another mentioned the Big Growl, and his heroism when the ground crumbled and the sky turned black.

But something was wrong. The wolf on the white stone was still alive! How could they stand there and talk about him as if he had already died, when he was still moving, his muzzle raised to the pale moon?

Finally, every wolf that was going to howl seemed to have done so, and as one, they turned and began to walk slowly back toward the lake and their camp. The elderly wolf stayed up on the rock, leaning his muzzle on his front paws.

But he's alive! Storm wanted to growl after them. *Are you just going to leave him here?*

It seemed that was exactly what they were going to do.

What about scavengers? Storm thought, her mind racing. *I've seen those huge birds circling near here, and I think I smelled foxes once! Even if they don't believe in Earth-Dog, it feels wrong to leave him there.*

It just seemed cruel.

The wolves were gone now, and Storm hesitated for a long

moment, before making her decision. Slowly, keeping her eyes and nose alert for any wolves coming back, she walked out into the plain and crossed to stand beneath the tall white stone.

"Hmmf?" the old wolf huffed, one eye opening and turning on her as she approached. There was a milky film over it, and Storm was sure the wolf was mostly blind.

"It's all right," Storm said softly. "I'll make sure you're buried properly."

"Have a heart, young . . . dog," croaked the old wolf. "I'm already dying. Find somewhere else to scavenge your next meal."

"I'm not going to eat you!" Storm whined, shuddering at the idea. She might have killed dogs and foxes before, but she was certain it would be wrong to *eat* something that was so much like her. "I want to make sure nothing else does eat you. I was watching, and I . . . I just didn't think you should have to do this by your-self. . . ." But Storm trailed off as the old wolf lifted his head, with some difficulty, and stared down at her. After a moment he let it fall back onto his paws with a sigh.

"Dogs," he muttered. "In my final hour, Great Wolf, you send me dogs?" He took a deep breath, and Storm could see his shoul-der bones moving under his loose skin. "This is the way of the wolf Pack, dog. Can't you see? When the Pack have said their good-byes, a wolf must walk to the moon alone."

Storm sat back on her haunches, a wave of sadness washing over her again. These wolves were so much like dogs, but so different at the same time. Could she really do nothing to help this poor old wolf?

"I can't just leave you here," she said quietly. "That's not the way of the wild—well, it's not *my* way. There are scavengers around, and you . . . you might not have finished your walk to the Great Wolf, before they come."

The old wolf growled, a sound like gravel rattling in his throat.

"Well . . . stay downwind, then," he said finally. "I don't wish to die with the scent of Longpaw Fang in my nose, thank you."

"*Longpaw Fang?*" Storm whimpered. "I knew a dog who used to call my kind that. But I'm not anybody's fang!"

The wolf's ears twitched, but he didn't reply.

Storm turned to walk a few paces away, though it made her sad to leave the wolf all alone. Then she paused and looked back.

"What's your name?" she asked.

The old wolf sighed. "I have no name," he said. "I have already gifted it back to my Pack." He looked at Storm, and for a moment there was a glint in his eyes—they were yellow again, and almost glowing as the moonlight shifted over his face. "One day soon, the name that was mine will belong to a cub. Now, I go by the name of all dying wolves. I am Fading."

"Fading," Storm murmured. "It was nice to meet you, Fading. And I . . . I'm sorry."

"Go away, dog," said Fading, but there was a hint of humor in his voice. "I must set out soon, and I believe it is quite a long walk." He looked up at the Moon-Dog, and the light faded from his eyes, turning them pale and silver once again.

Storm settled down a few pawsteps away, feeling like a great dog had hooked a freezing claw right through her chest. Was this really how wolves died? And what would the other dogs say if they could see Storm now, standing guard over a not-dog who didn't even really want her to?

She wasn't sure why it felt so important—but it was something she had to do. She thought back to the fox, the one that Sweet had told her to injure to send a message back to the other foxes.

Storm had refused. It had caused her all sorts of trouble, but she had seen that the fox was expecting cubs, and she couldn't do anything that would hurt an animal so defenseless, even if it was her enemy.

What *would* the Wild Pack say, if they could see her now, watching over a wolf?

She hoped they would see that she was a good dog—at least that she was trying to be.

Fading stopped breathing just before the Sun-Dog rose to begin his morning run. Fighting the urge to lie down and fall asleep, Storm wondered if she ought to bury the wolf after all—but if he really had to walk all the way to the Great Wolf in the moon, surely covering him with earth would be very unhelpful.

She padded closer to Fading's body already scenting the faint smell of death in the air around him as she reared up on her back paws, putting her front paws on the edge of the white stone.

"Hey!" barked a loud voice, and Storm half fell backward into the grass. She spun around and saw three large wolves pounding across the grass, their teeth bared. "Hey, scavenger dog! Get away from Fading!"

"I didn't—I'm not—" Storm began, but the wolves were closing in, and from the looks on their faces, she didn't think they would stop and listen to her tell them why she was here on their territory, intruding on their death ritual. She turned and ran, racing across the grass with her heart thumping in her ears.

"Get her!" another of the wolves cried. Their pawsteps were loud as they thudded across the grass behind Storm, and she tried to put on another burst of speed, keeping her head low and her ears pinned back. She felt like she was almost flying by the time she came to a copse of trees and slipped underneath a thornbush and through a tangled mess of vines. The thorns scratched at her short fur but couldn't get a grip. Behind her, she heard a crash of splintering wood and crunching leaves, and then a howl of pain and annoyance.

She dared to pause, hiding herself behind the huge trunk of a tree, and look back. The three wolves were all bigger than her, and they all had long, fluffy gray fur. Two of them had gotten stuck in the undergrowth when they'd tried to follow her through, and the third was pacing up and down in front of them, trying to nip at the thorns to untangle her Packmates. She stopped and turned, and for a moment Storm thought she would come after her—but then she just howled into the woods.

"Stay out of our territory, Longpaw Fang! We've scented you here before. Don't think we don't know about you!"

"Yeah, you and the others of your kind," growled one of the wolves who was stuck in the thornbush. "We know you're here. This is your first warning! If we catch you, you'll be sorry!"

Storm slunk away, as quickly and quietly as she could, until she was certain she was off the wolf Pack's territory. Then she sat down by the side of a trickling stream and took a long, cool drink.

What did they mean? she thought. *"The others of your kind"?*

Could they mean there are other dogs here? But they said Longpaw Fang . . .

That means there are other Fierce Dogs nearby!

CHAPTER FIVE

Storm was sniffing around the edge of a tangled thicket, trying to work out how she could catch the vole she was sure was living inside, when she picked up the scent.

It *was* a Fierce Dog scent.

The wolves' words had lodged in her mind, and she had spent a few days circling their territory, never getting too close, but searching for those other dog-scents they had mentioned. She knew they might have been mistaken, thinking that Storm's repeated visits to the edge of their camp meant there was more than one Fierce Dog around. Would wolves even know the difference between two Fierce Dogs' scents anyway? And what if *Longpaw Fang* meant something different to these wolves than it had to the old half wolf?

But here it was—a scent that wasn't Storm's own, but *definitely* belonged to another Fierce Dog.

Arrow?

Storm's heart leaped. Could it be? Arrow and Bella had headed in this direction when they had left the Wild Pack's territory. And they had even asked her to come with them.

I should have said yes. I should have just gone with them, two dogs I know mean me no harm and don't hate me just because I'm a Fierce Dog.

But as she investigated the scent, her nose skimming the forest floor, she realized she had been wrong to get her hopes up. This scent wasn't Arrow's. It was stronger, as if there were more than one Fierce Dog here, and there was no sign of Bella's scent, which had been fully intertwined with Arrow's by the time the two mates had left the Wild Pack territory.

This was a Fierce Dog *Pack*.

They had come into Storm's half-stolen territory, presumably hunting the same fat voles and weasels she had found between the tree roots.

I don't want to meet them.

After the battle on the ice and the death of Blade, the other Fierce Dogs had scattered, running for their lives. She tried to remember which of the dogs had died and which had run, but she couldn't. That day was a blur of snow, ice, and blood. She had been too exhausted from fighting to notice much else.

She had been lucky not to run into the Fierce Dogs before, when she was weaker. She didn't think hey would be particularly pleased to see her.

Storm hesitated, sniffing the air and getting her bearings. The pine trees rose high and dark all around her. If she continued the way she was going, following a ridge and the scent of prey, she would be going the same way that the Fierce Dogs had passed. She didn't want to go that way—but she had only two other options. She could retrace her steps along the ridge and almost certainly catch no more prey that day, or she could pick her way down between the trees . . . and back onto the wolf Pack's territory.

Her last encounter with the wolves had left her warier than before. Their furious snarling echoed in her mind long after she had escaped. If she truly thought of them as enemies, she would've been able to brave it, even knowing that it might come to a fight— but she didn't *want* to fight the wolves. They weren't her enemies, even if they didn't know that.

She would stay on her path. Perhaps she had missed the Fierce Dogs, and if not, it would be better to find out how many of them there were, so she could avoid them better in the future.

Satisfied with her conclusion, she padded on along the ridge, stopping every few pawsteps to scent the air. If she could stay downwind of the Fierce Dog scent, she might be able to see them before they knew she was there.

Storm moved through the trees a few quiet pawsteps at a time, as if she was tracking a particularly tricky piece of prey. She kept herself still and steady, pausing often to scent and listen for other dogs.

The trail led her down a slope and along the bottom of a gully, where a steady trickle of rainwater formed a tiny stream. The ground was muddy here, and the scent of both Fierce Dogs and prey was stronger—this was probably one of the places they came to hunt. Sure enough, Storm started to see tracks in the mud. Paw prints, the same size as her own, not the large and heavy pads of the wolves.

They led toward a patch of thick undergrowth where the valley widened out and the ground grew flatter.

Storm approached the bushes, the scent of other dogs rising all around her, hardly daring to breathe it in, in case her snuffling alerted the Fierce Dogs to her presence. One of them was here right now, just the other side of this thick tangle of twigs and leaves. . . . She would be very lucky to get past undetected.

For a moment the scent blinded Storm, not just with smells,

but with memories. She still wasn't sure which dog this was, but they smelled of *home*, in a way that made Storm's gut twist with confusion and anger.

The Fierce Dogs were never my Pack! I never lived in the Dog-Garden with the longpaws, and I never followed Blade.

But still, being so close to another Fierce Dog made Storm think of her litter-brothers, Wiggle and Grunt, of their scents when the three pups had huddled together for warmth and comfort in the Wild Pack's dens.

This dog isn't Wiggle. Storm shook herself. She couldn't let herself get distracted now. She needed to sneak past, as planned. The scent grew even stronger, and Storm felt panic rising, even as she tried to remain calm. Had she been scented? Should she break cover and run for it now?

Then another thought struck her:

This Fierce Dog is not Blade either. . . . Perhaps they would be willing to call a truce. She could explain that she was passing through, and they might not even care. No dog knew what the Fierce Dogs were like without their crazy Alpha.

There was another option. She could attack. Not to kill, but to scare them, to show that she was the dog to be avoided, not them.

"*You!*"

Storm spun around clumsily, one of her paws slipping on the mud.

A Fierce Dog stood behind her—*downwind*, she realized, just like she had been. It was a large female with black fur broken by a stripe of light brown down the center of her chest.

Pistol. Storm tried not to let her tail sink between her legs. Storm was so much bigger than she'd been last time they had met, and Pistol's fur was scruffy and thin. But still, Storm's ears tried to pin themselves back, as if they still belonged to the pup who had cowered from this dog's snapping teeth and mean words.

Pistol crouched, her lips drawn back to reveal fangs that were a little yellower but no less deadly. Storm tensed, ready to dodge if the other dog sprang at her throat.

"What are you doing in our territory, pup?" Pistol snarled.

"Our territory"? So there are at least two of them . . . how many more?

Storm flicked her tail in what she hoped was a dismissive way. "I'm not a pup anymore, Pistol. And I didn't know this was your territory," she said. "I was just passing through."

"You expect us to believe that?" growled another dog, this time from behind the thicket. The twigs parted as a dog crawled through a thin gap, and Storm had to take a few pawsteps closer to Pistol so that he wouldn't be right on top of her.

It was Dagger. He wriggled himself up and out of the bush and took a few more lopsided pawsteps toward Storm. Was he injured? He was limping, avoiding putting too much weight on his back right paw. But Storm couldn't see a fresh wound, only an old scar.

Is that from the battle on the ice? Did Lucky or I do that?

She couldn't remember which dogs she had fought that day and which she hadn't.

"Sniffing around right outside our den doesn't sound like 'passing through' to me," Dagger barked. He had seen her staring at his leg, and his hackles were raised. "Don't lie to us, little Lick."

Storm felt a shudder run all the way down her back as she looked from Dagger's angry face to Pistol's. They were flanking her, and the slope of the valley in front and behind would make it hard for her to escape.

"I *was* just passing by," she insisted. "I caught your scent while I was hunting, and I came to find out who was here. Now I know. I'll leave you alone."

"No," said Pistol. "You won't." She padded toward Storm, her steps silent in the mud. Her haunches were still taut, and Storm knew that Pistol might spring for her neck at any moment. Storm's heart pounded and she backed up the slope behind her, not letting the two dogs out of her sight—until her back legs bumped up against a large rock.

She was trapped. These dogs didn't want to run her off . . . they wanted to hurt her.

"What's the matter? Your precious Pack not coming to save you?" Dagger said, his tongue lolling in satisfaction. "Or have you come all this way by yourself? Still struggling to find a Pack that will accept a Fierce Dog outcast?"

"No dog likes a traitor, do they?" Pistol whined.

Storm felt the blood rising to her head, her vision blurring as she fought not to spring at Pistol.

How did she . . . ?

What? How did she know? *She doesn't! They're just trying to get under your fur. . . .*

She had to keep hold of her temper.

"It seems to me that it's more traitorous to follow an insane Alpha and kill your own Pack's innocent pups," she growled. Pistol and Dagger both growled back, baring their teeth, tensing to spring.

Pistol's only as big as me. Dagger's bigger, but he's injured.

If it had only been one of them, either one, Storm knew she could have won that fight.

But can I take them both? Can I fight off two full-grown Fierce Dogs?

I'm afraid I'm about to find out. . . .

CHAPTER SIX

Storm took a deep breath and pulled herself up as straight and strong as she could. The sharp eyes of Pistol and Dagger seemed to see right through her, but she kept herself still.

"I have no quarrel with you two," she said. "*Blade* was my enemy. She was the one who killed my litter-brothers, and she's gone. I don't need to fight you."

"Oh, but you do," snarled Pistol. "You killed our Alpha and broke our Pack apart. You and that filthy traitor Arrow. You are the enemies of all true Fierce Dogs!"

Storm tried not to react to Pistol's mention of Arrow, but a stab of panic had struck through her heart.

Please, Spirit Dogs, let Arrow and Bella have traveled far away, somewhere safe! If these dogs ever found them . . . or the pups Bella had been expecting . . .

Something told Storm that these dogs would not take the idea of Arrow having half-Fierce pups very well.

"The Earth-Dog must favor us," Dagger added, in a low and dangerous voice. "To bring you here alone and unprotected by those *Leashed* Dogs. Now, at last, Blade will be avenged."

They're talking as if nothing has changed at all, Storm realized. These two must have been chewing over the memory of the Storm of Dogs ever since, not really beginning new lives at all, even though they had traveled far away from the Wild Pack.

"We aren't at war anymore," Storm insisted. "The Storm of Dogs is over, and the world didn't end like Blade said it would! Why would you still want me as your enemy?"

I have a lot more reason to pick a fight than you do, she thought. *Your Pack abandoned us as helpless pups, killed our Mother-Dog, and then stood by while Blade tried to kill us all to fulfill some horrible prophecy that didn't even come true!*

But she *didn't* want to fight them. Storm tried to keep her voice from wavering with fear. "I would never have killed Blade if she hadn't tried to kill me first," she said. "Any dog would have done the same."

The dogs' expressions didn't change. All her words seemed to roll off their backs like raindrops. Storm's pelt prickled.

There's no way I can win this.

"And now you're in the same situation again," Dagger huffed. "Except that this time, there's no Leashed Pack to fight us for you while you sneak up on our leader like a coward—this time you have to face both of us!"

He lunged forward, snapping his teeth close to her throat, so close she could feel his breath on her fur. Storm winced but forced herself to hold still, even though her tail was quivering.

I will not show them that I'm afraid.

Pistol let out a volley of snapping barks right in Storm's ear, and Dagger paced back and forth, raking the muddy earth with his claws. Still, Storm held her ground. She stared back at them, hoping that they could not scent her fear.

They're trying to be like Blade, to make me dread the moment when they attack me. Like Terror, too.

I wonder if Blade ever heard of the Fear-Dog.

"I don't want to fight you," Storm said one more time, through her clenched teeth. Her legs felt soft now, useless in a fight, useless for running. "You don't have to keep doing Blade's work. We can make peace."

She didn't expect them to change their minds, but she felt that she had to try once more. Pistol and Dagger looked at each other and snarled, as if her suggestion had offended them.

"No peace!" Pistol barked.

"We will never have peace until we have vengeance!" Dagger roared, and launched himself at Storm.

It was real, this time, but Storm was ready. She ducked her head and leaped into a low dive. She heard Dagger hit the rock behind her with a thump and a yelp as the hard top of her skull collided with Pistol's chest.

Pain throbbed in Storm's head but Pistol fell back, snapping at Storm.

I hope that hurt you as much as it hurt me!

Storm rolled over on the ground and got up, backing away from both Fierce Dogs. Dagger was stumbling around to face her now, his good legs almost as wobbly as the bad one. He howled and fixed Storm with a mad stare.

Pistol shook herself and charged at Storm, and this time Storm couldn't dodge quickly enough. Pistol's jaws came down on her side, one fang tearing a long wound in Storm's fur. Pistol reared up, her front paws prepared to rake down across Storm's flank, but Storm twisted while Pistol was unbalanced on her back legs and managed to sink her teeth into one of them. Pistol convulsed and fell back, and Storm struck her across the jaw with one wild paw, cutting open her lip.

"Traitor!" Dagger snarled. Storm looked up—too late. Dagger bowled into her side, knocking her over. Mud and cold water splashed up in her face, and Storm tried to shake her head to clear her vision, but Dagger was on her, scratching at her sides.

She tried to ignore the pain and get up, but yelped and fell back as Pistol's weight joined Dagger's, both of them standing on her legs and raking her with their claws. Storm howled and snapped at the two Fierce Dogs, but they kept out of her reach. Panic filled Storm—she couldn't move and she couldn't *think*; there was mud in her eyes, and the Fierce Dogs' claws were like insects biting at her skin.

They didn't sink their teeth into her throat, though they could have. A shiver of fear crawled underneath Storm's fur. They were enjoying themselves too much to kill her yet.

They're toying with me . . . but I can use that.

She just had to figure out how.

"Does this hurt, traitor pup?" Dagger snarled, right into Storm's ear. "Pistol, I think little Lick doesn't like being scratched. Are you thinking what I'm thinking?"

Pistol huffed, as if he'd said something funny. Then Storm twitched as she felt jaws close on the back of her neck—but they still didn't tear at her. It was as if she was a tiny pup and they were picking her up. A horrible shiver ran down her spine.

I'm trapped!

They dragged her to her paws. She tried to shake the dogs off, but she couldn't get her balance fast enough to stop them—with a twist of Pistol's jaws and a hard shove of Dagger's shoulder, they threw her backward, into the thicket.

Now she understood.

The thorn twigs caught in her fur and dug into her skin. Storm yowled, high and pup-like even to her own ears. The Fierce Dogs stood back and watched, licking their wounds, their tongues hanging out in savage amusement. She wriggled, trying to free herself. With every movement the thorns bit deeper, but she couldn't stop—she wouldn't just hang there and wait for Pistol and Dagger to tire of watching.

She pulled herself, one stinging paw at a time, through the bush. Finally a tangle of twigs gave way and she fell from the thorns' grasp, landing in a clumsy heap on grass. By the scent, this must be where Pistol and Dagger slept. It was a sheltered grassy circle, protected by the thornbush and surrounded by trees and rocks and the steep sides of the small valley. A perfect camp . . . but small.

And there was no way out.

She shook her head, trying to finally clear the mud from her face, and staggered around to face her fate as she heard the rustling of the two Fierce Dogs picking their way through the bush behind her.

"Are you ready to die, little Lick?" Dagger howled.

"At last, you will join your litter-brothers, and Blade's prophecy will be fulfilled!" panted Pistol as she pushed out of the thicket, her teeth bared in a snarl of intent—and pain, Storm figured, for the two attackers had also been scratched by the thorns, though not as badly as she had.

Storm planted her stinging paws as firmly as she could in the soft grass. *If this is really where it all ends, I'll meet Wiggle in the Forests Beyond. . . .*

But then Storm remembered the time she had imagined she saw him, playing with Lucky and Sweet's pups in the Wild Pack, and fury flooded her chest. The edges of her vision flashed red.

No! I defeated Blade, and her false prophecy should have died with her. I won't be taken down by these lesser Fierce Dogs! I am a Fierce Dog too, and I'll fight for my own life!

A surge of energy coursed through her. She didn't wait for Pistol to attack. Instead she leaped, darting to the side and snapping

73

at Pistol's neck. The other Fierce Dog reared back, caught off guard, and scratched herself against the thorns. Dagger squeezed out into the clearing with a growl of anger.

Justice for Wiggle! Storm thought, throwing herself at Dagger, jaws open and slathering. She bowled him over and caught one of his ears in her fangs, and jerked her head back. His ear tore, and he howled in pain and anger. She snapped at him again, but he managed to roll away. Now, though, he was lying on his weak leg, and he struggled to get back upright. He looked at her with disgust, but there was something tired in his eyes.

"I'm going to kill you, pup!" Pistol barked, pulling herself free from the thorns.

Storm spun to face her, looking at the furious Fierce Dog . . . and at the hole in the bushes behind her.

I can't finish them both off. I don't want to. But if I can distract them . . .

Pistol was more cautious this time, circling Storm, snapping at her and trying to catch her ears and her forelegs without putting herself in range of Storm's own jaws. Storm turned carefully, watching, but always keeping herself between Pistol and Dagger. Finally, Pistol tried to duck under Storm's chin to sink her teeth into her throat, but Storm reared and twisted.

This was her chance. As she came down again, Storm kicked

out her back legs and fell, clumsily, onto the grass, her body tangling with Dagger's. She slipped onto her back, stretching out her legs, and let out a whimper—it wasn't hard to fake a hurt whine, since the wet grass was rubbing over the scratches across her back, making them sting. She twitched her back leg, as if she was struggling to get it under control. Dagger struggled beneath her, snarling.

Pistol took the bait. She lunged for Storm's leg, her jaws open wide.

Storm pulled away, exposing what was behind her.

Dagger's weak leg.

Pistol couldn't stop herself in time. Her jaws snapped shut with the full force that she had wanted to use on Storm, force that she'd probably hoped would break Storm's leg. Dagger howled. Pistol tore her fangs back from him and cowered, her ears pinned back in shock as she looked at the bleeding wound she had inflicted on her Packmate.

Storm shot under the thorns, through the bushes, out into the valley and away up the steep slope toward the forest. Her paws and her back still stung from the thorns and the Fierce Dogs' claws, but she focused on the top of the hill and pushed herself on. Behind her, Dagger's and Pistol's pained and furious howling echoed down the valley, but soon Storm was back among the trees. She looked back once, triumph and guilt fighting in her heart, but there was no sign of the Fierce Dogs. They weren't following her.

She turned into the forest and ran.

CHAPTER SEVEN

Where am I?

Storm's paws ached, and she sat down to lick at them, pulling pine needles from between her pads and trying to soothe away the places where the thorns had caught in her skin. The cuts had been bleeding, though they'd stopped now—she could feel the sharp taste on her tongue as she cleaned them.

It had started raining, a slight drizzle that sank into Storm's fur and made her feel shivery and cold. She hadn't dared go back to the territory she had made her own, now she knew that it was right between the Fierce Dogs' camp and the wolf Pack's strange longpaw-built valley. She had just run and run in the direction she had been facing when she escaped Dagger and Pistol, and now she was in another part of the forest, where the hills were fewer and the streams ran deeper and slower.

Storm sniffed the air carefully. The scents here were strange—the trees and the earth smelled the same, and she had scented the same prey creatures as in the other part of the forest. But here, there was something new . . . and something missing.

The salt is gone. She must have run farther than ever before from the Endless Lake, so far that its scent was no longer carried on the breeze. *But what else can I smell?*

There was wood in it, but dead wood, not growing trees. And also . . . something like smoke? But if the forest had been on fire, she would know about it. She had only seen fire before when Lightning had sprinted out of the sky and hit a tree in the Wild Pack's old territory, but if that had happened anywhere nearby, she was sure she would be able to smell it.

After she had soothed her paws for a little while, she got up and walked on, hoping that the flatter land might mean more fields where there might be rabbit holes. Sure enough, at one point she came to the edge of a line of trees and saw a wide grassy meadow in front of her—but it wasn't rabbits that she saw and scented when she looked across the field.

There was a longpaw den!

She froze on the edge of the open space, scenting the air. Now she knew that smokelike smell—it was like the one that came from the place where the longpaws were building their new structures, back near the Wild Pack camp. She took in an extra-deep sniff and tilted her head as she thought: the scent wasn't as strong here, but that made sense, because the den was much smaller than any she had seen before. It seemed like instead of hardstone, it had been made out of trees—she supposed that explained how she had scented wood and smoke, but hadn't seen a fire.

Even through the rain, she could tell that longpaw scent was all over this place. This was obviously their territory—but how far did it go? She looked around, wondering how long she would have to walk to be sure she was safe from the strange creatures. She would rather deal with the wolves than with longpaws—at least she knew where she stood with the wolves. Who knew what a longpaw would do? One might throw fire from a loudstick or trap her in a cage and make her drink poisoned water, while another might ignore her altogether, or bark at her in that strange, soft way, as if she were a Leashed Dog.

Then her stomach rumbled again, and she remembered what Lucky had said—*where there are longpaws, there's food.* Perhaps they had a spoil-box she could get into, if she was very careful.

She crept a little closer, across the wet grass, circling the small wooden den carefully. There was a hard-packed dirt road that led across the meadow, and a loudcage was sleeping on it, up close to the den. Storm spotted a box up against the wall that she thought might be a spoil-box and padded toward it, drooling. She could definitely smell longpaw food now. But there was something else too. . . .

A high-pitched bark sounded from behind her, then heavy, clumsy pawsteps on soft, slick earth. Too late, Storm made out the smell of dogs, and she whirled around. Was it the Fierce Dogs? Or the wolves? Had they followed her here?

For a moment, when she saw the two creatures approaching her, she thought it *was* the wolves. They were tall, with long, thick fur. Their faces were white, with shiny black ears and noses, and they had mottled gray fur all over the rest of their bodies. They had light blue eyes, like Moon from the Wild Pack.

But they weren't wolves. They only reminded her a little of them. In fact, they reminded her more of the half-wolf Alpha.

They couldn't be old Packmates of his, could they?

The two dogs pounded toward her over the grass, and Storm tensed, ready to run or defend herself, if necessary.

"Strange dog!" one of them barked. "What are you doing here?"

"Keep away from our longpaws!"

Our longpaws?

Storm looked closer, and now she could see why she hadn't scented them as she approached the longpaw den. They belonged to this place. Their scents were mingled with the longpaws'.

They were Leashed Dogs. Truly *Leashed*, with circles of brown hide around their throats, disturbing the flow of their thick fur.

Storm suppressed the urge to shift her weight nervously. She stood her ground even as the two gray-and-white dogs skidded to a clumsy halt a dog-length away.

"You're not supposed to be here, Fierce Dog," one of them growled, but her voice was slightly squeaky.

"You should leave, before we make you!" barked the other.

Storm stayed quiet and studied the two Leashed Dogs' wide eyes, and their paws that seemed too big for their bodies. They were quivering, and Storm couldn't tell if this was because of the rain, or for another reason.

They're still young, she thought. *They're younger than I am. And they've never lived in the wild, so they're not used to fighting . . . they're frightened of me!*

Storm glanced past the two dogs' nervously flicking ears, toward the wooden longpaw den.

"We're not afraid to fight you!" barked the female again, her

81

back arching as she shifted uneasily on her paws. "You should stay away from our home!"

"Our longpaws are big," the male growled. "And they're scary, and they're definitely not afraid of Fierce Dogs!"

The two young dogs were practically shaking from the effort of trying to seem unafraid. Storm wanted to back away submissively, to tell them that they didn't need to fight. She didn't want anything to do with their longpaws, after all, and the spoil-box wasn't worth having to wound two soft Leashed Dogs.

But behind her there was only the wooden wall of the longpaw den, and if she tried to run, the Leashed Dogs would almost certainly chase her. She could feel the tension in the air—if she gave any ground now, the boost to their fragile confidence might make them do something foolish.

"I was just passing by," she growled. *We're all reasonable dogs here.* "I don't want anything to do with this place. Let me pass!"

Too late, she realized the young dogs weren't listening. The female's growl was growing louder and more high-pitched, until she finally barked out—

"Alpha! Beta! Alpha Tom!"

Instinctively Storm backed away, and then growled again as she found herself wedged into the corner between the spoil-box and the wall. Two longpaws appeared around the corner of their den, sticks clutched in their hands.

They weren't like any other longpaws Storm had seen up close. Their strange-colored furs were red and black and blue, but they covered less of their skin than Storm had seen, leaving exposed hides around their arms and legs. Somehow, she didn't think this was a sign of weakness. They both looked powerfully muscular, at least as far as she could make out. One had a tuft of fur around his face, and the other was not as furry, but his hide was a darker color.

Their sticks were strange too—not loudsticks, Storm thought. They were long and silver, with one end that curved around and flattened into a sort of leaf shape.

"Alpha! A strange dog!" the male Leashed Dog half whined, turning his face to the longpaw with the face-fur. Storm tensed, ready to fight for her life if she had to.

But there was something about the way these longpaws were looking at her, and then at each other, and the way the sticks were held loosely in their paws.

If they were going to kill me, or drive me off, they would seem angrier. Wouldn't they?

She resisted the urge to growl and bark at them, her thoughts running faster and faster.

They must like *dogs.* She looked at the two young dogs, who were much more relaxed now their longpaws were here, looking up at them with their ears pricked up. The female's tail even wagged slightly as she waited to see what her Alpha would do. *These two pups seem happy, loyal, well-fed . . . if I keep still, perhaps the longpaws will just let me go!*

The longpaw Alpha made soft noises to the Beta, and then reached down and scratched behind the male dog's ears. Storm wanted to recoil from the gesture, but the dog wasn't afraid—in fact, he seemed reassured. She forced herself to stay still, keeping her ears and tail up.

The two longpaws lowered their sticks slowly, although they didn't drop them.

The Beta looked at Storm and made more noises—they were even softer, and slightly higher pitched. Storm was reminded of the noises that the longpaw had made to Mickey, when they had saved him from the great wave. Questioning, and inviting. Was he . . . trying to communicate with her?

"What's it saying?" she muttered. The female dog gave her a wary look.

"Beta Danny wants to know if you're a *good dog*," she said.

A third, high-pitched voice chimed in. "Tell him yes."

Storm looked around for the dog who had spoken. The voice sounded strangely familiar. . . .

Storm's eyes widened, and she sat back on her haunches in shock as a little shape trotted around the legs of the two longpaws. The top of his head barely came up to Storm's chest now, but his bulging eyes held the same cunning glint as they always had.

"Whine?"

Storm wanted to snarl at the little dog—the little *traitor*, who had sold the Wild Pack out to Blade and then vanished—but she caught herself. She couldn't do anything that would frighten these longpaws into attacking.

Whine was wearing a brown hide circle, too. Was he Leashed now?

"What are you doing here? I thought you were dead!" she said, lowering her head and hoping the longpaws couldn't tell she was on the edge of a growl.

"Buddy? Do you know this Fierce Dog?" said the young male.

Storm stared at Whine in astonishment. *Buddy? Is that your Leashed name?*

"Is—is she one of the savage ones?" the female asked tremulously.

No wonder they're afraid of Fierce Dogs, if they've been listening to Whine,

Storm thought, desperate to bark that she was *not savage!*

"No, Coco," said Whine. "She acts big and tough, but she's not dangerous. She wouldn't hurt you or Rex."

The two younger dogs immediately seemed to back down. They sat on their haunches, staring at Storm with friendly interest, all hostility apparently forgotten. Storm stared back in utter confusion.

The longpaw Beta noticed that Whine was beside him and gave a single alarmed bark, stepping in front of the little dog protectively. Whine's tongue lolled in amusement as he saw the expressions of confusion and anger pass over Storm's face.

"Listen to me, Storm," he said. "Do you want food? Or do you want Alpha and Beta to chase you away with their sticks?"

Storm was about to reply that she just wanted to get out of here, but then she realized she could still smell the food scents coming from the spoil-box, and her stomach rumbled audibly.

Betrayed by my own insides, she thought.

"All right then," she growled. "Say I did want food . . ."

"Do as I say," Whine said. "Lie down."

Storm looked up at the two longpaws. The Alpha took a cautious step toward her, speaking again in his soft voice, and she cringed away. "What?"

"Lie down on your side, and then show Alpha Tom your belly."

Storm glared at Whine. "That's crazy! I'd be . . ." Then she paused. She would be vulnerable. It would be just like showing submission to another dog.

Any longpaw that would take in Whine, *of all dogs, and give him a Leashed Dog name must* love *dogs,* she realized. *Maybe they're . . . kind? Maybe they'll feed me and then let me go.*

She looked into the eyes of the Alpha. It wasn't easy to read the strange, tall creatures—their ears didn't seem to move, their muzzles were the wrong shape—but he was leaning over toward her, making soft noises.

"Listen, I don't care what you do," Whine yapped, sitting down and scratching his ear with his hind leg. "I don't mind if the longpaws beat your head with those sticks after all. But if you listen to me, you'll be taken somewhere warm, out of the rain, and given food. Just let the longpaws think they're in charge."

Slowly, and with difficulty, as if her tense muscles were fighting against her decision, Storm lay down on her front and then flopped stiffly onto her side. She felt exposed and embarrassed, but the change on the Alpha's face was immediate, even if she couldn't quite tell what it meant. He bent his knees and put the stick down on the ground. Then he reached out a foreleg. Storm tensed, and she was about to roll to her paws when Whine yelped again.

"Don't panic," he said. "Just let them pet you."

"Let them what?" Storm huffed through her teeth. Then the Alpha's paw was coming down softly on her belly, stroking it while the Alpha made more sounds that she suspected were supposed to be comforting.

She tried to remember what Lucky had said about getting food from longpaws in the City, when he was a Lone Dog. *Look happy to see them,* he had told her, *like they're your best friends.*

She wasn't sure how to look happy so a longpaw would understand it. Especially since the longpaw was still "petting" her—it wasn't precisely unpleasant, just so *strange* that it made her skin crawl. Still, she let her tongue loll from her mouth and panted.

The longpaw took its foreleg away and stood up. It patted its knees and made a strange clicking sound with its mouth. Both Rex and Coco got to their paws as soon as they heard it.

"That means stand up," said Rex.

Storm got to her paws. "Like this?"

Part of her was howling with discomfort at the idea of following a longpaw's orders, but right now it was being shouted down by the rumbling of her stomach, and the sky was growing ever darker as the Sky-Dogs shrouded themselves with more heavy gray clouds.

The Alpha stood back and patted its knees again, and made some more noises. Storm looked at the Leashed Dogs.

"What now?"

"Go to him," Whine yapped. "He'll take you inside where the food is."

Storm walked forward. The longpaw kept going backward, and then he even straightened up and turned his back on Storm as he walked around the corner of the longpaw den. The Beta followed him, picking up both sticks but holding them in a completely different way, as if they weren't for hitting things with at all.

"He's trusting you to go with him," said Coco, her tongue lolling. "He's happy. He thinks you're a really good dog! Come on, it's this way." She and Rex both trotted after their longpaws, tails wagging, all their reservations about Storm apparently forgotten.

"Leashed Dogs are strange," Storm muttered as she walked carefully after the longpaws. The Alpha looked over his shoulder a few times and kept patting his back legs, as if checking that Storm was following him, but he did seem to be trusting her not to attack him or run off.

She stood at the doorway to the longpaw den and took a deep breath.

If she ran now, something told her that these longpaws and Leashed Dogs wouldn't chase her. She would be fine on her own—she always had been before. It was only a little more hunger, a little more rain.

Or . . . she could go inside this den, and she wouldn't have to get wet or hunt, just for this one day. She wouldn't have to be alone.

She stepped inside.

The smell of longpaws was overwhelming, a thousand different unfamiliar scents all swirling in the air around the small den. Underpaw, the ground was smooth and hard, but there were soft pelts lying on it too. Longpaw things were everywhere, most of them towering over Storm's head, strange shapes she couldn't begin to understand. In one corner of the den, there was a small fire! Storm recoiled from it, afraid, before she realized that somehow these longpaws had the flames under control—they were burning behind a sort of box made of black metal, and it didn't seem to scorch the wooden walls at all.

It was warm inside the den. Everything was dry. Storm felt herself begin to relax. Perhaps this had been a good decision.

Rex and Coco were ahead of her and the Alpha now, running through an opening to another part of the den. She could smell food in there, and her stomach rumbled again.

There were more longpaw things in this part of the den, but they smelled of earth. Several pairs of the strange paw-coverings they wore on their back legs, more of those silver sticks with the flat ends, two thin metal circles joined together . . . but also, three large silver bowls that smelled of Rex, Coco, and Whine—and of *food*.

The Alpha spoke softly to her again and reached up to a high place where a few brightly colored boxes were giving off the food smell that filled the air. It was delicious, but bizarre. Storm couldn't help herself drooling as the Alpha pulled down a box and a fourth silver bowl.

What kind of prey was in there? It wasn't rabbit, she was certain.

The Alpha tipped the box, and for a moment Storm thought she had been tricked. All that came out were pellets of some hard, brown substance.

But then she smelled them, and she knew—this was food. Leashed Dog food.

Is this what the Fierce Dogs used to eat in the Dog-Garden, before the Big

Growl? she wondered. *It smells . . . good!*

Rex, Coco, and Whine were all gathered around now, sitting down with their eyes pinned on their Alpha and their tails thumping against the smooth wooden floor. He made what Storm thought was a happy noise and poured out a little of the food pellets into the other three bowls too. The dogs immediately fell on the bowls and started to eat, noisily.

Storm took a cautious mouthful of the pellets. Then another. They tasted good, too.

The Alpha stood back and twined his long foreleg with that of his Beta, both of them watching Storm intently.

I'm no Leashed Dog, she thought. *I'm a Fierce Dog and a Wild Dog. You won't give me a name that isn't mine, or put one of those hide circles on me.*

But just for now, until the rain passed and she had filled her belly, she thought that perhaps some longpaws weren't so bad.

CHAPTER EIGHT

The forest was dark. Storm looked up, but she couldn't see the Moon-Dog, or a single star in the black sky—and yet there were no clouds, either. There was just an endless nothing, hanging over her head.

She padded between the trees, searching for something, though she wasn't sure what. There was no prey here, no little creatures to rustle in the undergrowth, no birds in the trees.

But she wasn't alone.

The other dog was nearby, no matter where Storm went. It was always right behind her. Sometimes she thought it had gone, but then there it was again. A presence, not moving, just nearby, always.

She spun, hoping to catch the dog behind her. There it was, a few trees away. An indistinct shape, watching her.

Who are you? *Storm tried to bark. The other dog didn't move or reply, but she sensed its malice. And more . . . its smugness. She couldn't see its face, couldn't even make out what kind of a dog it was, but she could feel the satisfaction it felt, watching her search the forest and never find what she was looking for.*

Leave me alone! *Storm howled, and she turned and ran, her paws pounding through the darkness. Before long, she slowed down again. She didn't know where she was going, and she was all alone. She would never find it this way.*

Then she realized that up ahead, and a little off to the side . . . the dog was still watching her.

She hadn't seen it move, and yet here it was.

This is why I left the Pack, *Storm growled.* To be away from other dogs, where I wouldn't be watched constantly!

The shadow dog didn't respond, but Storm knew it was enjoying her outbursts. She started toward it, but somehow by the time she reached the tree where it had been, the dog was gone. Storm turned slowly, and sure enough, the dog was sitting a few trees away, motionless but full of malevolent energy.

Coward, *Storm grumbled.* Why are you just *sitting* there? Come and do something! If you hate me so much, come and get me!

Or was Storm going to have to take the fight to it?

She fixed the dog in her sights. She wouldn't lose it this time! She sprang forward—

Something hard and cold struck Storm above one ear, and she startled awake with a yelp.

Where was she? What was happening? What had she hit her head on?

Oh, that's right. The cage.

She felt like a fool for trusting the longpaws. They had made the metal box seem so welcoming, full of soft things to sleep on and with a bowl of food and water, and she'd been so warm and sleepy, she had walked in willingly.

Then they had closed the door and locked it.

It was the morning now, the Sun-Dog's rays streaming through the high strips of clear-stone in the walls. Storm stood up, shaking herself to clear the last of her dream and the dizziness from bumping her head on the metal bars. She trod a circle among the soft hides and coverings, slightly resenting the fact that they had actually been comfortable. She could move a little, but not enough.

The three Leashed Dogs had calmed her initial panic, trotting freely throughout the den to show that the longpaws didn't capture all dogs and keep them in boxes.

"They'll let you out in the morning," Coco had promised, coming right up to the bars with a fearless smile that got on Storm's nerves. "It's only so you don't wander off or break anything. Rex and me, we slept in a box for a while, when we were pups! Buddy did too, when he first arrived."

Storm was not convinced. But she hadn't had much choice other than to trust them, though unease had never quite left her as she turned her sleep-circles and settled down.

I need to run. I can feel it in my paws, I've already stayed too long, and I can't spend another night in this cage. I won't.

Was this what it was like for Lucky and Sweet in the Trap House, before the Big Growl? The Trap House sounded like a terrible place. What would it be like to be surrounded by other dogs in cages just like this, frightened and cold? What if the Earth-Dog growled again?

She shuddered.

"You're awake! We're awake too," yapped Coco, bounding into the room with Rex on her heels. Storm bit back a sarcastic growl that she could see that for herself.

"Alpha and Beta will be up soon," said Rex. "Then they'll feed us and then we can go and play!"

"Beta takes us out in the mornings," Coco added, flopping down on her belly, her tongue lolling happily. "He always finds the best sticks."

They're like pups, Storm thought. *And not just because they're young. Is that what happens when you become a Leashed Dog? You don't need to hunt, so you just play all day?*

It almost sounded nice. Perhaps if a dog had never known anything else—or if Pack life had been no good for them, like Whine—it would be a perfectly good life.

But that doesn't mean it's for me. I don't want any longpaw telling me where I can go! I love to hunt and run. These two probably don't even know about the Sky-Dogs or the Forest-Dog.

Rex and Coco were pacing around the den now, sniffing things. For what purpose, Storm couldn't tell—surely they knew all this place's strange scents by now?

Coco stopped, looking up quickly, as Whine appeared through the opening to the next den-space. Then, to Storm's surprise, she bounded over and gave him a huge affectionate lick that unwrinkled all the folds on his face.

"Good morning, Buddy!" she yipped.

"All right, enough of that," Whine grumbled. Rex ruffed a hello as well, and Whine acknowledged it before padding over to Storm's cage.

Storm tried to draw back a little as the smaller dog approached.

Now that she was trapped, and not focusing all her energy on what the two longpaws were doing, she had a chance to really look at him properly.

He was a lot rounder than he had been when he was with the Wild Pack. Clearly, the longpaws weren't treating him like their Omega. Not that he deserved the title, Storm thought with a sniff. Sunshine was a better Omega than he had ever been. She didn't resent her role or plot and scheme to try to rise up the ranks.

Is that why he betrayed us? Because he was still bitter about being the Omega for so long?

"So, Storm," he said, as he came closer to the cage. "I never thought I would see you again, and that's a fact. What are you doing so far from the Wild Pack camp, anyway?"

I'm a Lone Dog now. Storm knew she should just say it and be proud, but the words seemed to stick in her teeth.

"It's not important," she said instead. Whine's bulging eyes gleamed, and Storm felt a growl start in her throat before he had even spoken.

"They didn't *kick you out*, did they?" he said, with spiteful delight in his yap. "After all that time Lucky spent defending you?"

"No. I chose to leave," Storm said. And it was true—but she couldn't seem to make herself meet Whine's eyes as she said it.

"Hah," Whine huffed. "Ungrateful. Half the dogs in that Pack would have died for you. Some of them *did*. And then you decided you'd rather be on your own? I always said you weren't to be trusted."

Storm twitched away from him, stung by his words.

It's not true, I'm not ungrateful, she thought. *They're the ones who changed their minds about me! It was the bad dog turning them all against me, that's all. There was nothing I could do.*

"Well, Lone Dog," Whine went on. "If you want to go back to hunting and being alone, you'd better pay attention."

Storm looked down at the little dog in surprise. "You're going to help me get out of here? Following your advice is what got me in this cage in the first place!"

Whine wheezed with amusement. "You think I want you to join this Pack? You'd only make trouble." He glanced behind him and lowered his voice so that Rex and Coco, who were rolling over on their backs and snapping at each other's tails, couldn't hear him. "I've got a good thing going here. A soft, dry den and plenty to eat, and you wouldn't believe how easy it is to get more. These two Leashed idiots are just like their longpaws, soft as mud and about as clever."

Storm had to shake herself to cover the laugh she had almost let out. It was strangely comforting to find that Whine was still his old scheming self.

"Anyway. In a while, the longpaws will come and let you out when they feed us, and then they'll put you back in the cage and take you in their loudcage to see the vet. That's what happened to me."

Storm frowned. She had heard of the vet. Sunshine, Mickey, and Daisy still talked about it sometimes, in low voices, whenever a dog was sick or hurt. The consensus seemed to be that the vet was a horrible place where they poked and prodded dogs and gave them horrible pellets to eat.

"But I'm not sick," she told Whine. "I don't need to go to the vet!"

Whine looked her up and down, blinking and sniffing. "You've looked better. What did you do to your fur, get in a fight with a pack of sharpclaws?"

Storm huffed.. "No." She could tell him that she fought off two Fierce Dogs, but that would only invite questions she didn't want to answer.

"They would take you anyway. That's what they do," Whine said, rolling his eyes. "Believe me. I've been through it. They take you to check that you're not hurt, and find out if you already belong to another longpaw—if you're a Wild Dog, or a lost Leashed Dog. See? All the vets know all the longpaws and their Leashed Dogs. Once the longpaws found out I didn't have a longpaw Alpha, they brought me to live with them."

"So what do I do?" Storm asked.

"You be a good dog," Whine said, his little floppy ears flicking in amusement. "Do everything a Leashed Dog would do. Then when they bring you back from the vet, they'll trust you. They'll take you out of the cage, and you can run off."

Storm eyed the little dog suspiciously. He wanted her to *let* the longpaws take her to the vet?

It occurred to her to wonder if she could trust him at all. After all, he had betrayed the Pack. He had hated Storm, so much that he didn't care if she lived or died. It was only because he'd seemed to give good advice that she had believed him so far. But it had landed her in this cage. . . .

Before she could growl her suspicions at him, the two Leashed Dogs suddenly jumped to their paws and barreled back to the cage, almost losing control and crashing into it.

"They're coming!" Rex barked, spinning around on bouncing paws. "I can smell Beta!"

"I'm *so hungry*," Coco yipped, standing by her empty bowl and almost shaking with excitement.

"When they let you out, we can eat and then we can play together! It's going to be *so much fun!*"

Storm sniffed. She couldn't make out any strengthening of longpaw scent from the confusing swirl of unfamiliar smells. But at the mention of food, she found herself starting to drool. Those Leashed Dog pellets were strange, and not nearly as satisfying as eating prey that you had caught with your own teeth—but they were tasty.

Maybe I should try to teach these two something about hunting before I go, she thought. *They're the first real Leashed Dogs I've seen since the Big Growl. What if they ever leave their longpaws, or there's another Growl? They look like they* should *be hunters, and they certainly can't rely on Whine to catch them anything to eat.* She shook the thought away. *They aren't my Pack. I don't have to take care of anyone.*

The door opened and the darker longpaw came in. He seemed to have changed the color and shape of his fur. Now it was yellow and green and covered all of his back legs. He had something in his hands. He patted his knees and called to Rex and Coco in that strange, lilting tone of voice. The Leashed Dogs immediately ran up to him, panting and wagging their tails. Rex turned another flailing circle on the spot, and Coco actually jumped up, as if she was going to sink her teeth into the longpaw's neck, but she just licked his face.

"The longpaws love it when we act like silly pups," Whine told Storm wryly, before running up to the Beta's feet and flopping down on his back, his round belly exposed and his legs sticking out at a thoroughly ridiculous angle.

The Beta leaned down and rubbed Whine's belly, and then ruffled the fur around the necks of the other two dogs. Suddenly, Storm realized that he had attached something to them both— thin strings that were part of the thing he was holding in his hands.

"Walk?!" Rex barked, as if it was the most wonderful thing that had ever happened to him.

"Yes! We're going on a walk!" Coco answered.

"I guess we're going out to play before breakfast today. Okay— bye, Storm, we'll see you later!" Rex yapped as the Beta led them through the door. They didn't seem to mind at all that the long-paw could keep them from running where they wanted!

Storm gazed after them in horror. "Why didn't he let me out?"

Whine shook his head and tried to scratch behind his ear, although his little back legs could barely reach. "Longpaws are strange. They're so predictable—except for when they're not.

They probably think you're not strong enough to keep up with morning patrol yet."

For a moment, Storm bristled, insulted. Why would they think that? She was a big, strong dog, twice as strong as either Rex or Coco—wasn't she?

Then she looked at Whine, who was panting with the effort of getting his back paw behind his head.

"Why didn't they take you?" she asked, cocking her head to one side. "Is it because *you* can't keep up?"

Whine growled. "And what's wrong with that? I've got short legs, and I'm not as young as I used to be."

"I think you're up to something," Storm bit back. "You've always been sneaky. Maybe I should stay with this Pack, make sure that you're not plotting against those two good pups."

Whine sighed and shook his head. "All I'm plotting these days is how to get into the food boxes and blame it on Coco. Don't look at me like that," he said, when Storm's ears flattened and she bared her teeth. "Nothing will happen to her. The longpaws love them. They love me too, although I can't work out why. It's not like a Wild Pack here. Even if you break the rules, the punishments are never worse than having to sit outside for a while."

Whine seemed to give this some thought for a moment, and

then he licked his chops with his long pink tongue.

"Anyway, I want you out of here, believe me. I'm not having you turning Fierce and messing this up for me. The sooner you leave, the better."

Storm suppressed a growl. *I am* Fierce, she thought. *I don't* turn Fierce.

"I'm not going to the vet," she said, as calmly as she could. "Who knows what they'll do to me there? Is it true that they stab you with long thorns?"

"Yes," said Whine with a shudder. "And sometimes it's worse than that. Coco went to the vet once, and . . ."

"What?" Storm prodded him, though she wasn't sure she wanted to know what was so bad that even Whine didn't want to talk about it.

"She had to live with them for a few days, and when she came home, they had cut down a patch of her fur right to the skin and made a cut as long as your paw, and then mended it again."

Storm's jaw dropped. *"Why?"*

"Who knows why longpaws do things?"

"I'm not going, Whine. You have to help me get out of here before they take me."

Whine trod a circle, clearly torn between not wanting to do

what Storm told him to do and wanting to get her out of his cozy longpaw den. Finally he nodded.

"I have an idea. But we'll need Rex and Coco. When they get back, we'll get to work."

Storm settled down in the soft blankets in the bottom of the cage and rested her chin on her paws.

There was nothing to do now but wait. She hated waiting. She tried to stop her mind from racing around, chasing visions of longpaws with sharp thorns holding her down. . . .

When Rex and Coco came back, they were panting, and Storm could smell the fresh scent of the outside world all over them. Rex had a twig stuck in his tail.

How hard did the longpaws make them run? she wondered. *I always thought no longpaw could keep up with a dog.*

She was hoping that the Beta would let her out of the cage and feed them now, but he just made some more noises to the Leashed Dogs and went back to the other part of the den, shutting the door behind him. Rex and Coco flopped down on one of the pelts on the floor, their tongues lolling and eyes starting to blink closed.

"Don't go to sleep!" Whine yapped, bouncing up to them.

"Come on, get up! Storm needs your help."

At that, the young dogs' ears pricked up, although a little less quickly than before.

"Help? Why?" Coco yawned. "Are you sick? Should we get Alpha?"

"No!" Storm said quickly. "I just need to get out of here."

"You mean you're not staying?" asked Rex, his ears and tail drooping. Storm was strangely touched.

"Do you . . . really want me to stay?"

"Yes!" Rex yipped. "You're a good dog. Beta says so. He likes you. So we like you too."

Storm huffed. If only life in the Wild Pack had been this simple.

"Storm needs to go," Whine told them. "She needs to get back to her own Pack. They miss her."

Storm's heart felt as if a vet was stabbing one of their long thorns into it. She glared at Whine, who glared back with one bulbous eye. *He's saying this to get their help. Not to make you feel bad,* Storm thought.

. . . probably.

"You pups don't know," Whine said, "but being in a real Pack . . . it's a very special feeling. Having a bond with so many dogs . . . it's like you've all made a promise that to keep each other safe. It's having somewhere you will always be wanted."

"You'd be wanted here," Coco told Storm, putting her fore-paws on the cage. "We would keep you safe!"

"But she already has a Pack," said Rex slowly. He frowned. "Imagine if we got lost and found our way to Storm's Pack—we would want to come home to Alpha and Beta, wouldn't we? Even if the Pack promised we could play all day and chew on anything we liked?"

"Of course," Coco said. She thought about it for a moment. "Yes, of course. I understand now."

"So, first we need to get Storm out of this cage," said Whine. "Rex, I need you to do that trick we've been practicing."

Rex looked worried. "But it's Bad. Alpha was really upset last time. . . ."

"You won't get in trouble, I promise," Whine wheedled. Storm wondered if that was true.

"Oh all right," said Rex. He trotted up to the door on Storm's cage and carefully grabbed a bit of the metal between his teeth. Storm backed away, wincing, as he wriggled and chewed and his teeth scraped against the surface. Then suddenly, one of the pieces moved, and the cage door swung open.

Storm bounded out, shook herself from head to toe, and then stretched hugely, reaching her front paws out as far as they would go.

"Agh, that's better!" she yipped happily. Then, as she scrambled to her paws, she gave Rex a suspicious glare. "Why didn't you say you could do that?"

"It's a bad dog trick," Rex said sheepishly. "I should only do it when Buddy says so."

Storm caught Whine's eye, and he looked away quickly. *There's only one bad dog in this household, Rex,* she thought, *and it's not you.*

But in the end, she was glad that he was here, causing trouble for these silly dogs and their silly longpaws, rather than out in the wild, where he could do real damage. It looked like Whine had found his place in the world. Storm hoped she could find hers too.

And I never thought I would need Whine's *help to do it!*

"What now, *Buddy*?" she asked him.

Whine turned his squashed face up, and she followed his gaze to a high-up piece of clear-stone in one wall, where light was filtering into the room. Storm could see that there was a tiny gap between the clear-stone and the wood. "They leave that window a little bit open, to let the outside scents in," he said. "All we need to do is give it a push."

Storm went over to the clear-stone and reared up, walking her front paws up the wall until she was stretched out as tall as she could go. "I'm not going to be able to reach it."

"I can help," said Coco. Storm backed off and tilted her head at the dog—she was not quite as big as Storm. How was she going to get up to the window? But instead of trying, Coco lay down against the wall with her paws braced on the ground. "I can make you taller!"

Storm eyed her skeptically. "Are you sure? I'm not exactly a small dog."

"I can do it," Coco panted. "As long as you don't stand on me for very long. You'll have to move quickly."

Storm's heart suddenly felt full of warmth for these two dogs. Even Whine had turned out to be far more generous than she had expected. She licked Coco's wolfish face in gratitude, then turned and nuzzled Rex, and then Whine, nipping playfully at the little dog's wrinkled neck.

"Thank you," she said. "I won't forget any of you." She reared up again, putting her front paws on the wall, and then stepped gently onto Coco's back with her hindpaws. The boost was enough that she could just get her nose onto the clear-stone. She pushed it, and it flapped open. Outside, the smell of pine and grass and rain was strong and fresh.

Her back legs wobbled as Coco got up to her paws. The young dog's legs shook once, and then she braced them and held still. Storm put her paws up over the ledge and glanced back one last time at the Leashed Dogs, looking up at her with sad eyes but wagging tails. Then she pushed off Coco's back and scrambled, clawing at the wooden wall with her back legs and wriggling herself up and out through the hole. It wasn't dignified, and she bruised her belly on the sharp corner of the wall, but finally she was dropping down outside, and her paws landed safely on the soft, muddy ground.

She broke into a run at once. The longpaws might have heard her; they could be back any moment! And besides, after a long night in a longpaw cage, her legs were itching for a good run. She streaked across the grassy meadow, kicking up little pieces of mud as she went, feeling the wind pulling at her ears.

She didn't know where she was going, but she looked up and saw the same strange scene as before. Behind the trees, the ground grew in points, reaching up into the sky. *I'll head that way,* she thought, as she darted under the canopy of the forest. *If I know where the Endless Lake is, and where the High Ground is, I'll never be truly lost.*

Storm ran as fast as she could through the maze of tree trunks, until she was certain that the longpaws wouldn't follow her so far. Then she slowed to a happy trot, enjoying the feeling of the needles beneath her paws and the scents of prey. Her belly rumbled again. She wished that the longpaws had fed her before she'd escaped, but she was looking forward to a hunt and the warmth of fresh-caught prey. She felt as if she had been in that cage for days and days, instead of just one night.

Something suddenly rustled in a nearby bush, and Storm jumped as a small bird took flight, flapping away in a panic.

Just a bird, Storm thought—but it had stirred another memory, one she hadn't given much thought to when she was still in the longpaw den.

In her dream, she had been walking through a forest, and something had been watching her, stalking her . . . *laughing* at her.

She shook herself. She was certain that the Fierce Dogs hadn't followed her, and that the wolves wouldn't bother her if she wasn't on their territory. There *was* no dog here to worry about.

She was all alone, again.

Despite the joy of being out in the world, and the prospect of real prey and even the idea that she might find out what was on the High Ground . . . there was a strange feeling in Storm's belly.

A prickling sadness that seemed to grow heavier and heavier with every step she took away from the longpaw Pack. She slowed and stopped, looking back over her shoulder toward the meadow and the wooden den.

Don't be silly, she chided herself. *You don't want to go back there! They'll take you to the vet. They'll make you patrol on a string and sleep in a cage. And you'll have to spend all your time with Whine.*

But even Whine suddenly didn't seem so bad. After all, he'd been part of a Pack once.

That was it. And now Storm could see that this heavy feeling had been building all this time. It went away when she was with the wolves, or when hunting was going really well, but it was always there.

I don't want to be a Leashed Dog. I just miss my Pack.

They were mean and distrustful and they never listened to Storm, even when she was right. But they could be kind and loyal, too, and if only the bad dog hadn't kept making them think she was plotting against them . . .

Storm sat down on her haunches and howled.

"I can't go back! They'll never take me back. And why would I want them to, after what they've done?" she growled to the sky.

But then what would she do? Lone Dog life was too hard, too

lonely. She knew that now. Would she just keep walking until she stumbled across a dog Pack who would take her?

No. There's no need. Hope sprang up in Storm's chest. *There are two dogs out there I know would want me in their Pack.*

I just need to find them.

CHAPTER NINE

The Sun-Dog was going down, its reflection glimmering on the surface of the Endless Lake as Storm emerged from the tree line.

She had walked all day, almost nonstop since she'd left the longpaw den, using the Endless Lake and the High Ground to guide her steps, and there had been no scent or track marks that would lead her to Bella and Arrow. Her hope from earlier had disappeared almost as quickly as her extra energy from a sheltered night and good food. How had she expected to find Bella and Arrow? How many territories would she have to search? She could walk forever and never find them.

She shook off these thoughts as her stomach rumbled. She'd managed to catch a small weasel in the forest earlier, but it hadn't been enough for a whole day of walking. It was time to hunt.

I never thought I'd want any part of a Leashed Dog's life, but a bowl of those strange pellets would be very tasty right now.

She stepped once more onto the sandy ground at the edge of the lake, looking up at the wheeling white birds that nested in the rocks along the bank.

They're so big, she thought. *I bet they're delicious. But they have their guard up all the time! How can I get close enough to catch one?*

Another of the plump birds circled overhead and let out a squawk that sounded annoyingly like a taunt. She watched as it flapped down and started pecking at a dark shape that looked like it had washed up out of the lake. It looked like something that had once been alive, but a long time ago. Would these birds eat almost anything, as long as it didn't fight back?

I wonder . . .

She took a few unsteady steps forward, and then let herself slump down in the sand. She lay perfectly still on her side, resisting the urge to wriggle to get more comfortable, and shut her eyes.

If they think I'm dead, maybe they'll come and try to eat me, and I can get my teeth into one then. . . .

But playing dead was difficult. She knew that her breath was moving the sand in front of her face, but if she tried not to breathe, then she would die for real. She couldn't smell whether the birds were coming, so she had to try to keep looking convincingly dead.

Then she shuddered, sending grains of sand skittering away from her. An image had passed across her vision.

Whisper.

His body, the way they had found it in the woods . . . the limpness in his legs, the tongue lolling from his mouth, his eyes open and staring . . .

She leaped to her paws and shook herself hard, sand flying all around her. She couldn't do this. It didn't feel right, somehow.

I'm sorry, Whisper.

Storm started to run, following the line of the Endless Lake. She barreled through a flock of birds, making them scatter. If she only had hind legs like a sharpclaw—Lucky had told her once that they could jump many times their own height—but she didn't, and she wouldn't waste any more time here trying to catch these stupid birds. She would keep moving until she scented prey that she *could* catch.

And she wouldn't think about Whisper. Or about his killer, the bad dog, who Storm had never caught. Who she was still running away from, even now.

She had crested a small hill of sand and thick pale grass, and as she looked out across the water, she could see a blocky shape silhouetted against the last of the Sun-Dog.

"Another floatcage," she muttered, thinking of the longpaws she had seen getting in and out of one of those, back near the Pack camp. "More longpaw stuff."

Lucky had said that before the Big Growl, this was all longpaw territory, from the big City across the river to the Light House, and probably much farther. Was this their territory too? They could move such huge distances so easily in their loudcages and floatcages and loudbirds.

Is there anywhere that's not *longpaw territory?* Storm wondered. *And what if they want to take all of it back? Where will the Wild Pack go then?*

The Wind-Dogs were running faster now, whipping up the surface of the lake and blowing the floatcage from side to side.

Storm's nose twitched, picking up a scent.

Is that . . . Fierce Dog?

She felt hope leap in her chest. It was familiar, but so vague, and the salty tang of the lake was so strong, she just couldn't be sure. Even if it was a Fierce Dog, she was close enough to the forest that it could be Pistol or Dagger instead of Arrow.

Still, she wouldn't run away from it. She wouldn't let those two stop her from finding a Pack where she could belong.

She followed the scent along the beach. Her paws sank into the sand, the wind blew more sand into her eyes, and her whole body felt heavy with hunger. Storm plodded on as the Sun-Dog sank lower in the sky. She wondered briefly if she should turn inland to hunt, but then she worried that she would lose the scent—it was almost completely gone already. She couldn't bear to give up even the smallest chance of finding Bella and Arrow.

The last lingering light of the Sun-Dog faded around her.

She knew she couldn't keep walking all night, so she turned and walked up the beach a little, onto a rocky slope that led down to the water. The Moon-Dog was already bright in the sky. Her silvery light combined with the sound and smell of the lake was strangely comforting. It was so familiar, and it truly did seem to go on forever.

Storm sniffed around the rocks until she found a cool cave just large enough for her to curl up inside—it was dry and had grass growing around its mouth. She hoped that meant she wouldn't wake up with the lake lapping at her nose. She turned a tight sleep-circle and settled down with her muzzle resting on her back paws.

I wonder what the Wild Pack are doing now, she thought, as her eyes drifted closed. *Or Arrow and Bella. I wonder if I'll ever see any of them again.*

* * *

Lucky frowned at her with worry. "Turn around, let me see where it hurts."

Lick obeyed, scuffing her paws sheepishly as she showed him the scratches on her shoulder.

Lucky shook his head and licked them gently. It made them sting a little less.

"You need to control that temper of yours," Lucky said. "It'll get you into trouble one day."

"Grunt started it," Lick mumbled. "It's not my fault. He always plays rough. What should I do, play dead?"

"That's enough," said Lucky, which Lick noticed was not an answer. He went back to licking her scratches.

She sniffed. There was something strange about the scents in this place. She could smell the Endless Lake and cool earth, but also . . .

"Lucky, can you smell that?" she asked.

Lucky huffed into her fur, as if he was annoyed by the question. "Don't distract me right now, Lick."

"But I mean it," she told him. In frustration she stepped away from him, nudging his muzzle away from her with her nose. "There's a dog! A strange dog, coming closer! Can't you smell it?"

"Don't be silly!" Lucky growled. "You're always making things up."

"I don't make things up," Lick growled back. "You just never believe me. Why don't you ever listen?"

"That's enough, pup!" Lucky backed away. "If you're going to make trouble, *you can stay out here until the Pack decides you can come back."* He turned and walked away from her, vanishing slowly into the darkness.

"Wait, Lucky—there's a strange dog out there! It's not safe!" Lick tried to follow him, but he was gone. *"Lucky, don't leave me here . . . don't go . . ."*

Storm woke up with a start, her heart racing. For a moment, she peered across the sand in the weak early light, looking for Lucky. Then she realized that their argument had only been a dream.

The Fierce Dog scent was still there, hanging in the air, still frustratingly too weak for her to be certain whether it was Pistol and Dagger, or Arrow, or even some other survivor of the Storm of Dogs.

Whoever it is, I won't let them sneak up on me this time. She was going to look for them, and if she found herself in another fight, so be it. She was hungry, but still strong.

She left the cave and looked around at the stretch of lakeshore. The Sun-Dog was still in his den, but she could already see his light. Soon he would poke his head up above the trees behind her. To her left, she knew she could follow the line of the Endless Lake and she would come back to the broken longpaw place, then the Light House, and then the Wild Pack's camp. To her right was a mystery, except for the faint Fierce Dog scent.

She set off, determination in every step, the sand shifting under her paws.

I'll need to find prey soon, she thought. *I could head into the trees and come back here after I've eaten.*

But she still didn't like the idea of losing the scent—she had a horrible feeling that it would evade her again if she let it go for a moment. So she ignored the hollow feeling growing in her stomach and walked on, climbing a ridge of rock that rose above the sand. She knew she could cope with hunger a lot worse than this. She sniffed the air every few pawsteps, and the Fierce Dog scent did, at last, grow stronger and stronger.

Soon she realized that she must be within the dog's territory, or at least somewhere it had stayed for a while. The scent came and went, more recent trails overlaying older ones. On one tree it would seem as if the dog had been gone for a long time, but a few pawsteps later it was as if it was right behind her.

She turned carefully, determined not to get trapped again.

It smelled like it might be Arrow—but if it was him, why was it only his scent she could find?

She felt her heart start to beat faster as her excitement mingled with worry.

If Arrow is here, where is Bella?

Bella could have left Arrow alone, or been hurt, or died. . . .

She stopped and shook her head, trying to clear that thought out of her mind.

She skirted the edge of a huge rock that reminded her of the overhanging boulder on High Watch, where she had been sent as a punishment when Sweet found out she had disobeyed orders and spared the fox. Where Bruno had been killed.

She fought a shiver of guilt. "It wasn't my fault," she growled, as if she could scare away the gray, sad spirits of the Bruno and Whisper before they started to follow her. "I'm sorry, but I didn't do it!"

It didn't help. In fact, the farther she walked, the more she felt like she was being watched. The Fierce Dog's scent kept getting stronger and then fading again, almost as if . . .

Is it here, following me?

She wheeled to face the trees, scanning the landscape. With the Endless Lake behind her, it wouldn't be able to creep up on her. She'd had enough of this. If she had to fight this dog, she would fight it on her own terms.

"Hello?" she barked, as loud as she could. "Come out! I know you're there!"

She thought about adding that she was looking for her friends, or that she didn't want to trespass on some other dog's territory—but she stopped herself, waiting to see what the dog would do.

"Storm?" came the reply.

Storm's heart gave a huge lurch of relief as a pair of pointed ears appeared over a rocky ridge, and then the rest of Arrow bounded into sight.

I can't believe it! I found him!

Storm hardly dared to trust what she was seeing. But her joy was suddenly marred by a stab of worry. What if he wasn't pleased to see her? What if she was an unwelcome reminder of the Wild Pack? Sure, he and Bella had invited her before, but things might have changed. Storm thought back to her sleepwalking. Things had *definitely* changed.

Arrow gave a bark of joy and thundered down the slope toward her. "Storm! It's really you!"

Storm stood and watched him approach, too overwhelmed to move.

He's happy to see me. He really is happy I'm here!

A heavy feeling in her belly was starting to lift, one that she hadn't realized was there until it was suddenly gone. She'd never thought, for all her determination, that she would really find Arrow, and yet here he was.

"Storm, what are you doing here?" Arrow cried, bounding up to Storm and licking her nose. "You're a long way from the Wild Pack camp! Is Lucky with you?"

Storm felt herself bounding and leaping in response as she returned his licks.

"No," Storm said. "I—I've left them. Like you did. You and Bella said I could join you. . . ."

The Fierce Dog just stared at her, his joy gone—now he just cocked his head in confusion. Storm almost flinched at his narrow-eyed gaze. *Please don't make me talk about it,* she willed him silently. *It hurts too much, and it'll only make me so angry.*

She stared back at him, waiting for his reaction.

Please ask me to stay.

Arrow looked Storm up and down, and a low whine escaped his throat.

She braced herself.

If he doesn't want me, I'll be fine. Lucky was a Lone Dog.

Arrow's expression was solemn, and Storm's tail drooped between her legs. "Storm, all these scratches—the Wild Pack didn't . . ."

"Oh! No, no, I didn't fight them. I just left," Storm assured him.

I wouldn't fight my own Pack. You know me. Please, Arrow.

Arrow suddenly seemed to notice her anguish. "Storm, of *course* you can stay with us. We would be honored to have you in our Pack." Storm felt all her muscles relaxing as giddy glee rushed through her body.

"Oh, thank you, Arrow! Thank you! I promise I will be a good dog!" Storm felt like a pup again. All exhaustion was forgotten as she gamboled in the sand, whining happily.

Arrow wagged his tail, but his face was serious. "But Storm, I'm worried about you. You look thin. You must have been traveling a long time. I didn't even recognize your scent at first. I thought it might be Pistol or Dagger!"

"Oh, so you've met them," Storm said, stiffening up again just at the mention of the Fierce Dogs' names and flicking her ears in distaste.

"Not face-to-face, thank the Watch-Dog," said Arrow. "Bella and I scented them as we were traveling and stayed well clear, but I sneaked around and spotted them hunting."

"They gave me these scratches," Storm said, licking at her paw. The scratches had hardly bothered her since she'd spent the night with the longpaws, but she guessed they must look worse than they really were. "Anyway, where's Bella? Is she all right? I didn't scent her on the way."

"She's fine," Arrow said, and a look of dopey happiness came over his face. He looked so silly, but so content, Storm couldn't help huffing at him with amusement. She would never understand what made dogs want to be mates, but she was glad it made Arrow so happy. He seemed almost like a different dog, nothing like the stressed and angry Packmate she remembered, always closely watching his own behavior in case he was accused of being a traitor. "She can't move much right now, so I'm hunting for two. And more than two! The pups are coming soon! I'm going to be a Father-Dog any day now. Come on, let's get back to her. She'll want to see you."

Arrow turned to lead Storm over the ridge and into the trees, and Storm felt another rush of relief. It was so nice just to be able to follow another dog, one who knew where they were going. To walk into territory where she was welcome! She barely paid attention to where he was leading her, happy to trot after him, sniffing around for prey nests that she might come back to, enjoying the warm glints of light from the Sun-Dog through the trees as he poked his nose over the horizon.

It feels like coming home, even though I've never been here before.

Suddenly, Arrow stopped and sniffed the air. He made a

thoughtful noise in the back of his throat and then turned left, away from what seemed to Storm to be a clear path, and splashed through a small stream before heading up a steep scrubby bank. Storm sniffed, wondering what had made him take this particular route, and a familiar scent prickled through her nostrils.

"The wolf Pack!" she said. When she thought about her position and the direction they'd traveled, it made sense—they must be somewhere on the other side of the wolves' territory.

"Have you run into them too?" Arrow asked.

"Kind of," said Storm. She didn't want really to talk about all the times she had snuck slightly too close to watch them, or her encounters with Thoughtful or Fading. Not right now. Perhaps when they got to Bella, she would tell them both everything that had happened.

"The edge of their territory is just through those trees. They don't bother us," Arrow said, "but we keep away when we scent that they've been exploring up here. After all, there are only two of us. Well, three now," he added, with a slow, happy blink in Storm's direction.

Storm's heart swelled, and she splashed across the stream in two long bounds to join him on the bank.

"There's plenty of prey, and we were worried the wolves might want to keep it for themselves," said Arrow. "But so far they—"

He was cut off by a terrible sound, the howl of a dog in pain. Storm's ears flattened against her head, and she saw Arrow's long-paw-cut ones do the same.

"Arrow! Arrow, where are you?!" the dog howled.

Storm looked at Arrow, wide-eyed, but he was already running. She leaped after him, following the awful howling.

It was Bella.

CHAPTER TEN

Arrow raced ahead, as if the Fear-Dog was at his heels, and Storm soon lost sight of him. She tried to keep up, but her paws were stiff and sore from her long journey, and she hadn't eaten for a day, so he quickly outpaced her. All she could do was run as fast as she could, following the sounds of Bella's distress, and tell herself that as long as Bella was howling, she was still alive.

She tried to ignore the warring worries in her heart. Could it be the wolves, or the other Fierce Dogs? Or worse . . . could the bad dog have followed her here?

Finally, Storm scrambled up over a large rock and slid down into a clearing in the forest. In the middle of the grassy space, Bella was lying on her side, with Arrow beside her. Storm sniffed for enemies, but she couldn't smell anything but the two dogs.

"It's happening," Arrow said, and for a moment Storm didn't

know what he was talking about. Then Bella took a labored breath, and Storm saw her swollen belly, and realized.

"The pups are coming?" she gasped.

Bella looked up and saw her, and there was excitement in her huge, dark eyes as well as pain.

"Oh Storm . . . I'm so glad to see you! When did . . . *agh*." She fell silent with a swallowed sort of whine.

"Can you get into the den?" Arrow asked, his tail between his legs but still wagging hard. Bella struggled to her paws. Storm ran to her and put her head beneath the golden dog's shoulder, taking some of her weight. Bella gave Storm a grateful lick on the ear as between them, Storm and Arrow steered her into a hollow, deep underneath a thick gorse hedge. The den had been filled with moss and leaves. It looked comfortable—and just big enough for two dogs.

"I'll be right outside," Storm said quickly, "if you need anything." She didn't know the first thing about birthing pups, and the idea of being so close to Bella while it happened gave her a funny, shuddery feeling in her paws.

Arrow shot her a grateful glance. "Thanks, Storm. I'm glad you're here."

Storm nodded to him, and then lay down in the grass to wait.

She couldn't stay settled for very long. The noises coming from the den were too alarming. Although Sweet had made all the same noises when she was birthing her pups, and Storm was sure Bella and the pups were going to be fine, it was hard to relax in a new place with those kinds of sounds hanging in the air. She began to pace, first patrolling the edge of the grassy clearing, investigating all the new smells. Then she wound through the trees, never far enough that she couldn't get back to the den in a few bounds, but exploring Bella and Arrow's camp. It was nicely placed, down in a hollow so it would be sheltered from the wind and the worst of the rain. She started looking for a place where she could sleep and found a bush that might be suitable.

The Sun-Dog passed overhead, and for a little while the camp was full of deliciously warm light. Storm tried to enjoy it while it lasted, but she couldn't make herself relax.

She knew that it could be a long while yet, and she couldn't pace the entire time, but her paws seemed to think she could. They were full of nervous energy.

I won't be able to relax until the pups are born, she thought. Then, *Oh, it must be so much worse for Arrow . . . and how must* Bella *feel?*

"Storm?" Arrow called suddenly, and Storm leaped to attention, wagging her tail. Could the pups be here already? "Can you go and fetch Bella some water?"

"Yes!" Storm barked, delighted to have a job to do. "I'll be right back!" She went straight to a place where she'd found some lovely thick moss, tore off a large chunk, and scrambled up the slope, heading toward the stream that she and Arrow had crossed over.

As she was dipping the moss into the nice cool water, she thought, *I wonder what Sunshine would say if she could see me. I'm an Omega now too!* Storm felt a rush of affection as she thought of the fluffy little white dog. She knew most dogs would balk at the idea of being the Omega, but somehow she felt that would be disloyal to Sunshine. Besides, what could be more important than taking care of your Pack?

As the Sun-Dog trotted slowly toward the Endless Lake, Storm made it her business to keep returning to the stream for fresh water, and to go into the forest to look for more comfy moss to bring for Bella's den. She even caught a shrew, and instead of eating herself, insisted that Arrow come out of the den, stretch, and eat something.

It's going to be strange being the third dog in a Pack of three, she thought. *This Omega thing isn't so bad.*

It helped to have something to keep her mind off the

birth—or the lack of birth. The longer Bella's labor went on, the higher-pitched and more painful her whines and howls seemed to become.

Lucky and Sweet's pups had taken a while to arrive, but not this long. Storm tried to stay calm, for Bella's sake, but she found herself digging little holes in the grassy ground, for no reason except that she could. She tried to clean her scratches, but after a while she had licked one of her paws so much it was getting more sore, not less.

The Sun-Dog vanished, and darkness fell. Suddenly, the unfamiliar territory seemed threatening, and Storm found herself patrolling the camp again, and then standing at the mouth of Bella's den with her ears pricked up, staring into the dark, challenging any wolf or giantfur or longpaw or *anything* to try to get to her. Nothing came, and the tension began to make Storm's head ache.

Eventually Bella's howls eased off, as the Moon-Dog rose in the sky, darting in and out of the clouds as if she was as restless as Storm was. A weak, silvery light filled the camp, so Storm could see the pain and worry on Arrow's face as he emerged from the dark den.

"Something's wrong," he said. "The pups haven't come, and

Bella's getting so tired, she can't even howl anymore. . . ."

"I don't know how to help," Storm whined. "What can we do?"

Arrow wasn't looking at her. His eyes couldn't seem to focus on anything at all. Storm noticed that he had a patch on one of his legs where his fur was slightly thin, as if he'd been grooming it all day, just like she'd over-groomed her own paw.

"I don't know," he said, to no dog in particular. "None of us know anything about birthing pups!"

The terrible irony of it struck Storm like a blow from Lightning.

If we were still with the Wild Pack, we would be surrounded by dogs who knew about this—Sweet, Lucky, Moon, even Sunshine would be able to help us.

She could fetch and carry like a good Omega, but she was a big strong dog, a hunter at heart, built for chasing down prey and defending her Pack. If they were under attack from a giantfur, Storm would know what to do. But what use was she in a situation like this?

Arrow was probably feeling the same.

Storm glanced back at the den mouth. It was so dark in there. Were those ordinary shadows, or . . .

No, I won't look for signs where there aren't any. If the Earth-Dog has something to say to me, she'll speak more clearly.

The night was passing quickly. The Moon-Dog was gone, but the clearing was still filled with an eerie light. Soon the Sun-Dog would be back. He slept so little during Long Light.

Storm felt sick with worry about Bella. If she had eaten prey recently, she was sure she would have brought it back up by now. They had to *do* something, but what? She hadn't stayed awake all night since the time she tried to stop herself from sleepwalking by keeping herself from sleeping at all. She was starting to feel the same horrible mixture of tiredness and jittery energy. She tried to think, but her mind was fuzzy.

"Why aren't they coming?" Bella whined, weakly, from the darkness. "Please, Earth-Dog . . ." She broke off with another pained howl, but Storm knew what she was thinking.

Please, Earth-Dog, don't take her . . . don't take the pups.

Now Bella's howl was growing louder—so loud, it hurt Storm's ears. How could any dog bear such pain? Bella would not last much longer like this.

I must do something, anything!

An idea crept into Storm's mind. "We need help," she called, over the noise of Bella's cries. "And the Spirit Dogs can't help us now. But I think I know who can." She gave Arrow a hard lick on the side of his face, hoping she could give him some strength.

"Hold on, Bella, I'm going to look for help!" she barked, and scrambled away, as fast as her stiff legs would take her.

"Storm! We have no friends near here! Where are you going?" Arrow barked after her, but Storm didn't stop to answer.

She couldn't tell him. She couldn't get his hopes up. It had taken her all day to even think of it herself, but now the hope burned in her heart like the Sun-Dog.

There's one creature nearby who's been friendly to me.

Thoughtful!

Storm splashed across the stream, and the cold water on her paws gave her a burst of wakefulness. The wolf scent began here, and she followed it, skidding as she swerved to avoid trees and rocks, running as hard as she could and pushing herself to go faster. When she was surrounded by wolf scents, certain she was deep in their territory, she raised her muzzle to the dawn sky and howled.

"Help! I need help!"

There was a faint growl in the distance, and Storm headed right for it, knowing that her only hope was to find a wolf, any wolf, and see if she could persuade them to let her talk to Thoughtful. It was a foolish thing to do, but she had no choice.

She suddenly came out into a wide, clear space. After a

desperate moment of staring around at the meadow in front of her, and beyond it sheer cliffs with ragged, square edges, she realized she was at the bottom of the longpaw-carved valley. Up above, on the far side of the valley, she could just make out the white path that led to the Dead Tree, and her old camp. To her left there was the high rock where she had met Fading, and on her right, the flat grassy bottom of the valley and the lake.

She heard heavy pawsteps and scented wolves, but she couldn't see them. She started to turn, and then something smacked into her ribs, knocking her right off her paws and sending her sprawling in the grass.

She scrambled upright as quick as she could, but by the time she had, she was surrounded by wolves. They seemed to have come out of nowhere, or out of the fading darkness itself. Five of them, all huge, bigger than Storm by at least three or four paw-lengths, and all of them growling so low and angry that the sound vibrated almost painfully in Storm's head. Storm's ears pressed to her skull and she tried to look around without meeting any wolf's eyes, afraid of provoking them. None of them were Thoughtful . . . but one of them was the towering Wolf Alpha. She stepped forward, forcing Storm to shuffle back so her tail was almost within snapping reach of the wolves' jaws.

"What do you mean by this, little dog?" she snarled, in a voice that Storm thought could scare the seabirds off the cliffs from a hundred rabbit-chases away. "You are a spy, and a thief—yet you have come onto our territory and howled for our attention. Why?"

I'm not— Storm thought, but she stamped the words down. There was no time to protest.

"I need help," she barked, trying to sound desperate, but not afraid. She hadn't felt small in a long time, but right now she felt like a pup again, trying to justify herself to bigger, scarier dogs. "My Packmate's life is in danger, and—"

"No," said the Alpha.

Storm's heart sank like a stone. She wondered, could she say she just needed Thoughtful to come help? But she couldn't be sure she wouldn't be getting the kind wolf in some sort of trouble with his Alpha. Still, she tried—"Please, I know you have no reason to help us, but *please* . . ."

"We do not go running off before sunrise to help *dogs* with their problems." The Wolf Alpha swished her tail. "Do not come here again."

Without the Alpha giving any signal that Storm could see, the two wolves on Storm's left sprang. She tried to dodge them, but there was nowhere for her to go but into the jaws of the wolves on her right. She tripped and fell onto her side. The wolves quickly pinned her with their big, heavy paws. She writhed and tried to bite them, panic overwhelming caution, but it was no good.

The Wolf Alpha placed a paw on Storm's flank. She felt the claws digging into her fur, and howled in frustration and fear as the Alpha scraped along the skin. Then she and the other wolves drew back.

Storm got up, gasping, the scrape stinging horribly. Emotions fought inside her like a couple of angry sharpclaws. She had failed. But she was alive.

"Never come into our territory again. This is your second warning," said the Alpha, and lunged, snapping her jaws shut just a paw-length or two from Storm's nose. She flinched away, but far too late. If the wolf had meant to hurt her, she would have.

The Alpha snorted and turned away, and all the wolves trotted after her, not looking back. They didn't even stay to chase Storm off their land.

They think I won't try to stay, Storm thought. *They think I'll be too afraid.*

They weren't wrong. Storm tried to turn and run back to Bella and Arrow.

I've failed. I left them all alone for nothing.

Although her heart was pumping as if she was racing across the ground, she couldn't manage much more than a slow trot. Her legs were shaking too much. She went as fast as she could, feeling devastated that her plan hadn't worked, worried that when she got back something terrible would have happened.

Then she heard pawsteps behind her. Another wolf. Probably sent to make sure she left, after all.

I'm going! she thought, in a panic, and tried to run faster. She didn't turn back. They might see that as another attempt to talk, or even to get back into their territory.

"Wait, Storm," came a soft bark, and Storm stumbled to a halt and turned.

It was Thoughtful. He was following her, but keeping himself half-hidden among the trees. *Hidden from his own Pack,* Storm realized. He nodded to her and cast a shifty glance down the valley toward his Pack's camp.

"I heard you. I'm sorry about the others. We enforce our borders, no excuses, no matter how harmless the outsider—that's just how it is. You're lucky you were only on your second warning."

Storm stared at him, confused.

She didn't think she had ever in her life been called "harmless." From her very first days with the Wild Pack, some dog or other had always thought that she was dangerous, trouble, just because she was a Fierce Dog, no matter how small or how scared she was deep down.

It was disorienting to talk with a creature who thought a grown Fierce Dog was no threat to them at all.

"Your Alpha wounded me," she reminded him balefully. The cut was stinging. It was deep and ran across several of the barely healed scratches she'd received from Pistol and Dagger.

"Yes, but not badly . . ." He shook his head, speaking quickly and quietly. "If you break the Great Wolf's rules, you will be given four warnings, one for every season of the moon—each stronger than the last. This was your second. If I were you, I would make sure I didn't get to four."

Storm tried to take all this in, but she couldn't focus. It sounded like nonsense to her. In fact, it sounded like he was telling her that she could break the rules one more time without being punished.

Wolves are so strange, she thought.

"But never mind that now. What happened to your friend?" Thoughtful asked. "What kind of help do you need?"

That snapped Storm out of her puzzlement, and she whined. "My friend is having pups—I mean, she's trying, but it's not working. It's been a whole day! None of us know anything about birthing pups, and we don't know what to do. Is there any wolf in your Pack who knows about pups, who would help us?"

Thoughtful sighed. "I'm no help. But my sister-wolf would know what to do."

"Your litter-sister?" Storm asked, her ears pricking up, pathetically grateful. "Would she help us?"

"I think so. Peaceful is our Healer, and she earned her name with honor. She rarely leaves camp. But she hates the idea of *any* creature suffering unnecessarily. I will send her to you. She can make her own decision. Wait here," he said, turning and dashing away.

Storm let herself sink down on her belly and watched him go. Distantly, she marveled at how the wolves could cover so much ground so quickly, and in total silence when they wanted to.

In the hush that followed, Storm could hear the faint sound of Bella howling in pain and terror. Storm put her muzzle down on the ground and covered it with her paws.

O Spirit Dogs, I've tried to be a good dog. I've tried so hard. Please help her.

She appealed to them in turn, in her head—Earth-Dog, the huge black dog that saw every dog's life and death; Forest-Dog, who loved the cunning and the hunters; the Sky-Dogs, changeable and contradictory litter-siblings; River-Dog, steady and loving but dangerous too. The Wind-Dogs, who would run forever, and Thunder and Lightning. . . .

Then there was the Watch-Dog.

Storm knew that Arrow believed in him. It was a Fierce Dog belief, but one she had never learned. She thought of the dream she'd had of Whisper, lying contentedly in the Wild Pack camp, and the enormous Fierce Dog shape that had blotted out the Sun-Dog's light. He was the dog that knew everything, that witnessed every thought in a dog's head, good or bad, and stood in silent judgment.

Watch-Dog, if you are there, I appeal to you now. Help Arrow. Help his pups to live. . . .

"Hello, dog?" came a whimper from the darkness, and Storm almost whined aloud in surprise. But it wasn't the Watch-Dog. A slim, light gray wolf with one white ear came padding through the trees.

"Peaceful?" Storm guessed.

"Yes," said Peaceful. "My brother-wolf tells me there are pups in danger. Is this true?" Her voice was like the other wolves', deeper than most dogs, with the resonance that gave Storm the feeling she could make herself heard from very far away. But she was hanging back from Storm, giving her a chance to look her up and down, and Storm could see the same quiet kindness in her eyes as she had seen in Thoughtful's. She felt that she could trust the wolf.

Before Storm could answer the question, though, another faint howl of pain floated through the air, and Peaceful's demeanor changed completely. She stiffened, raised herself to her full imposing height, and her ears twisted up and back.

"Oh no," she said. "Take me there. We must go *now*."

Storm didn't need any more encouragement. The wolf's alarm was enough to set her heart pounding again, and she broke into a run, hope flaring in her chest once more. Peaceful kept easy pace with her, her strides almost twice as long as Storm's, and they seemed to cross the distance between the wolf territory and the hollow in no time at all.

"Arrow," Storm gasped, over another howl from Bella. "I've brought help!" She skidded to a halt outside the den. The Sun-Dog was waking up, and Storm could see a little way into the den. Arrow turned and scrambled out, and stopped when he saw Peaceful, his hackles raised.

"Help?" he growled. "From a wolf?" He spread his stance, protecting the mouth of the den, ready to fight. Storm's fur shivered along her spine, and the Wolf Alpha's scratch stung her again. No Father-Dog would normally let another creature near his mate at a time like this, let alone a wolf. But if any dogs knew how dangerous it was to judge a creature by their appearance, it was Arrow and Storm.

"Please," Peaceful said, dropping her shoulders, almost submissively. "I'm my Pack's Healer. I can help your mate and her pups if you'll let me."

The anger ebbed away from Arrow's stance, but he didn't move.

"I . . . I think one of the pups is . . . stuck," he said, through gritted teeth. "Can you help her?"

Peaceful dipped her head. "I know what to do, if you will let me in."

Slowly, stiffly, Arrow stood aside. Storm wanted to go to him and lick his ears and tell him he'd made the right choice, but she was so full of hope and worry she could barely breathe. Peaceful slowly squeezed into the den, murmuring to Bella that it was all right and she was here to help, not hurt her. Arrow followed, even though he had to stay in the entrance with his back legs still outside.

Storm curled up nearby and started trying to lick the scratch the Wolf Alpha had given her, but twisting her neck to reach it stretched her fur out and only made it sting more, so she had to leave it alone. The sky was brightening now, and the Sun-Dog was on his way. Birds twittered in the branches of the trees above them, completely unaware of the desperate drama unfolding in the den below. Storm found herself up and pacing again, the same pattern, crisscrossing the clearing.

By the time this is over, I'll have worn down all the grass, she thought.

Bella's howling stopped, and then started again, and then stopped. Peaceful was doing *something*. Storm truly did not want to know what it was.

Finally, Bella gave a great yelp that sent all the birds in the trees scattering, and then she fell silent. Storm held her breath, feeling like she was standing on the edge of a cliff. . . .

"It's out!"

Storm barked and bounced on her paws, as if she was a pup again herself.

A pup had been born! Her tail wagged so hard it smacked against her legs. She was filled with relief. She didn't know what to do with herself. She wanted to meet the pup, but there was no room in the den, and she shouldn't bother Bella now. There should be more pups on the way. Storm hoped that they were a little more eager to be born than their litter-sibling.

"It's all right," she heard Peaceful say. "Good, Bella. Rest, if you can. It's all right."

Storm lay down and finally felt as if she could stay there for a while. Peaceful's voice was so soothing, she even found her eyes drooping shut.

Thank you, Spirit Dogs.

Everything is going to be all right.

CHAPTER ELEVEN

Bella howled again after the first pup was born, but there was less pain in her voice, and almost no panic. The sound wasn't exactly restful, but Storm knew that it was natural, and that Peaceful was there to help if something went wrong. Finally, when the Sun-Dog was peeking into the clearing over the tops of the trees, Bella's howls stopped. There was a muttered conversation from the den, and then Arrow emerged and walked over to Storm.

"It's over," he said. He flopped down beside her. He looked like he was going to say something else, and then stopped. "Storm, you're hurt."

"The Wolf Alpha caught me, before I found Peaceful," Storm said, trying to make it sound as incidental as she could. Arrow didn't need anything else to worry about, now that he was a Father-Dog. "It's just a scratch."

"It looks sore."

"I can't reach to clean it," Storm said, and twisted her neck to demonstrate, and then regretted it as the wound stung her again.

"Here." Arrow licked at her flank, smoothing down the fur and soothing the soreness.

Storm felt a warm rush of happiness. It was lovely to be in a Pack again. She'd almost forgotten what it was like to have another dog casually help her.

"Is Bella okay?" Storm asked him. "What about the pups?"

"Bella is fine," said Arrow. "Peaceful's helping her now. I can't thank you enough for bringing her here, Storm. You saved Bella's life."

Storm bent her head, happy but slightly anxious. "I didn't do much. We were lucky she was willing to come."

"Still. You ran straight into wolf territory for us. I'll never forget it."

A prickling feeling of unease suddenly started up between Storm's ears.

"Arrow, what about the pups?" she asked again, trying to keep her tone light. "How many?"

Arrow sat back on his haunches and sighed.

"Two. Two healthy male pups." He took a deep breath. "They

had a litter-sister . . . the first to be born, the pup that was stuck. She didn't survive."

"Oh, Arrow." Storm scrambled to her feet, paused awkwardly for a moment, and then rubbed her head against his shoulder. "I'm so sorry."

"Thanks, Storm," Arrow whined.

I was too late, Storm thought, feeling sick, as if she'd eaten prey that had gone bad. She knew that Peaceful had saved Bella and the two living pups. But to finally birth a pup, and then find it had died . . . it seemed so *cruel*.

She couldn't help thinking of her own brothers. Both murdered by Blade, in the end—but Fang had made his own choices, at least, whereas poor little Wiggle . . .

We were so small, she thought. *So defenseless. Barely any older than Bella's pups, really.*

She pulled away from Arrow and shook herself from head to paw, trying to throw off the memories. It was no good wishing that things were different. Not now.

"Come and meet them," Arrow said.

"Are you sure?" Storm asked.

Arrow nodded and wagged his tail, though his eyes still looked a little sad. "Bella wants to see you. Come on." He led her over to the den and went inside. Storm followed him, afraid it might be too much of a squash. But the den was a little bigger now, with a pile of sticks by the entrance where either Peaceful or Arrow had broken off the twigs from the underside of the hedge to make a larger space.

The den smelled of blood and exhaustion, and something Storm had only faintly smelled before, when Lucky and Sweet's pups were born. Arrow nuzzled Bella and settled down beside her, while Peaceful fussed about, rearranging the bedding around Bella.

Bella herself was lying on her side, her muzzle resting on the moss and her eyes almost closed. Her golden fur was puffed up, tangled with moss and twigs. And cuddled tightly to Bella's side were three little bundles of wet fluff. Two of them were black, and as Storm watched, they wriggled, trying to get closer to Bella, opening their tiny pink mouths. The third was sandy-colored and lay perfectly still on her side, almost as if she was just sleeping. Bella nuzzled all three of them, licking them in turn, the two living pups and their litter-sister who had already gone to be with the Earth-Dog.

Storm let out a soft whine, despite knowing she should stay strong for Bella's sake. It didn't feel fair. How could two of the pups be here, their tiny sides vibrating with their first breaths, when the third was already gone?

"Poor pup," said Peaceful gently, in that rumbling, soothing voice. "But this, too, is a part of life and motherhood. Not all litters survive the journey to the living world together."

Bella looked up at her, grief and exhaustion in her eyes.

"Two of my cubs died," Peaceful said quietly. "From my first litter. It's a hard truth, but these are the truths that bind us, as mothers and cubs, and as Packs."

But if this happens often . . . Storm shook her head. How could dogs bear it? And then she thought of Lucky and Sweet. *Four pups, and they all made it, even if Tiny was a runt to begin with. He really was lucky that day.*

A different sort of sadness washed over her, as she thought of those pups—of Tumble, Fluff, Tiny, and Nibble. They would be growing up into big, strong dogs now. By next Ice Wind, they would even have chosen their names. It hurt, more than she had ever expected, to think that she wouldn't be there to see it.

But these new pups will need me too, she reminded herself.

Slowly, with one eye on Bella, Peaceful reached down and took up the motionless sandy pup by the scruff of her neck. She moved her to the edge of the den, apart from the others. Bella whined and stretched out one leg, but then she drew it back, tucking it protectively over the two little, warm black bundles.

"This little one has simply gotten a head start on the rest of us, in our journey to the moon, to be with our ancestors," Peaceful murmured.

Storm glanced at Bella and Arrow. Bella hardly seemed to have heard her, but Arrow's head tilted in confusion.

"Peaceful," Storm said quickly, "Dogs don't go to the Moon-Dog. We go to be with Earth-Dog. We'll bury the pup, and that way the Earth-Dog will be able to take her to the Forests Beyond."

With Wiggle, Storm thought. *And Martha.* The thought was painful and good, all at once. *Martha will know what to do. She'll look after her.*

"Really?" said Peaceful quietly. "But . . . dogs do howl to the moon, don't they? Are you not howling to your ancestors?"

"No," Storm said. "The Great Howl is . . . it's to bring the Pack together, with all the Spirit Dogs." *Perhaps it would be nice to howl to the Forests Beyond,* she thought, *but I don't know how we could.*

"Well. Perhaps the Great Wolf and the Moon-Dog are friends. They both watch over us, after all."

"I hope they are," said Bella hoarsely. "If so, then Moon-Dog is very fortunate to have a wolf for a friend. I will never, ever forget how you helped us, Peaceful. I hope one day I can return the favor."

Peaceful bowed her head, her large ears turned back. "It was a joy to have helped bring these two precious cubs into the world," she said seriously.

As if they heard her, the two black pups at Bella's side both wriggled and let out the tiniest squeaking noises Storm had ever heard. They opened their little pink mouths again and mewled.

"The cubs are hungry," Peaceful said. "Bella, you know what to do now. Come, Storm. Let us leave the new parents to tend to their litter."

Storm stood and awkwardly shuffled backward out of the den. Outside was bright and cool, after the cozy dimness of the den, and Storm sprawled, exhausted, on the grass. Peaceful sat beside her, and then stretched out her front legs and let out the hugest yawn Storm thought she'd ever seen.

"It's a nice idea," Storm said. "That wolves go to the moon when they die. But I'm not sure how it works."

"What do you mean?" Peaceful asked.

"Well . . . dead animals go into the ground," Storm said slowly. "Even ones that aren't buried. Eventually, they fall apart and they go into the earth. That's how we know Earth-Dog takes dogs when they die. So what about wolves? Did Fading's body not go into the ground?"

"Hmm," said Peaceful, and Storm suddenly realized that perhaps she shouldn't have mentioned Fading. Would Peaceful be angry, knowing that Storm had intruded on the death of a Packmate? "My brother-wolf told me he thought it was you who'd been seen with Fading. I don't know why you did that, but now that I've met you, I don't think you meant any harm."

"I didn't! I wanted to make sure that scavengers didn't disturb him, before he . . . before it was over," Storm said. "Fading said that he was going to the Great Wolf . . . but his body stayed up on the rock."

"But wolves don't stay with their bodies when they die," Peaceful said. "Do dogs?"

"Well . . . no," Storm said. "So I guess . . . dogs and wolves live differently, so perhaps they go to different places afterward too."

"That's a good way to look at it." Peaceful tilted her huge gray head. "Do you know, Storm, not many creatures would accept the ways of others as you have. Especially not dogs. You aren't as stubborn as some of your kind."

Storm dipped her head in gratitude, but she knew that it was true. Some dogs could be incredibly insistent on an idea, once they had gotten it into their heads.

Like the Fear-Dog. It felt wrong to even think about him, in this sunny clearing, with the two innocent pups enjoying their first feed so close by. But some of Twitch's old Pack—*Terror's* Pack—had held on to their belief that the Fear-Dog was real, and that the whole Wild Pack should be afraid of it. Even perfectly rational dogs like Breeze refused to accept that Terror had invented the Spirit Dog himself.

"I suppose, when you are already an outcast from most of your own kind, you can see others' points of view," Storm muttered. "I was born into a Fierce Dog Pack—a Longpaw Fang Pack, as you might call them—but I never belonged there," she finished. She couldn't go into the whole story of Blade's Pack, the terrible prophecies, the Storm of Dogs. "It must be much harder to do what you did. You must have been with the wolf Pack all your life—and yet you still came to help us. It was very brave of you. And very kind."

Peaceful blinked slowly, and Storm could tell that she was pleased.

"I wanted to do what was right," she said.

Arrow emerged from the den, and Storm's heart lurched as she saw that he was carrying the sandy pup loosely in his mouth.

He laid her down gently on the ground.

Out here in the light, Storm could see that she was the same color as Bella all over except for a little ring of black fur, right on the top of her head.

I've never seen a marking like that before, she thought.

"Bella's sleeping now," said Arrow. "So are Nip and Scramble."

Nip and Scramble, Storm thought, a rush of fondness warming her from the middle of her chest. *Welcome to our Pack, little ones. I'll watch over you, just like your Father-Dog and Mother-Dog. . . .*

"Bella . . . Bella has said her good-byes to Tufty." He nuzzled the little shape at his paws, and Storm held back a sad whimper. Tufty was a lovely pup name. "Now it's time we buried her. We'll keep her close. So we can keep an eye on her."

Storm and Peaceful both rose and followed Arrow as he carried Tufty over the lip of the hollow. He looked around, and then he picked a spot where a bright patch of sunlight lit up the forest floor.

"Here," he muttered. "So you won't get cold."

Storm stepped forward and began to dig in the sunny spot, and Peaceful joined her. It barely took any time at all—they only needed a tiny hole, for such a small dog.

Storm's heart ached. *It's so unfair, to die before you really live.*

Arrow gently lowered Tufty into the grave, and there was a long silence.

The Alpha or Beta would normally say something, Storm thought. *But I don't suppose Arrow and Bella have even thought about which of them is which—in a Pack of two, that sort of ceremony probably didn't seem important.*

Something told Storm that Bella would be the Alpha, anyway—she had wanted the role before, when the Pack had chosen Sweet, and Arrow had never shown any sign of wanting a greater rank than he had as a hunter.

But now, Storm could tell that Arrow wasn't sure what to do. He looked at her, and she gave him a tiny encouraging nod. *You can do this.*

Arrow sighed and hung his head.

"When . . . when we left the Wild Pack, we had a vision of a new way. A Pack where it doesn't matter what kind of dog you were born. Nip and Scramble will grow up in that Pack—but you won't have the chance, Tufty. It hurts." He took a deep breath. "But this Pack won't always be easy. There will be problems, and dangers, and some other dogs will distrust your litter-brothers, even though they've never hurt anyone, just because of who their Father-Dog is. And I'm . . . glad that you won't have to know what that's like.

159

"I wish you had stayed. I wish that you'll know how loved you were. Your Mother-Dog and I are sorry we'll never see you grow. We—we know you would have been a good dog."

Storm turned her face to the sky and whined in grief-filled agreement.

Arrow fell silent for a moment. Then he stepped forward. "Now you go to the Forests Beyond, where it is always Long Light and the prey is plentiful. Good hunting, Tufty," he said, and scraped a pawful of earth down over her little body.

Storm followed. "Good hunting, Tufty," she said. *Earth-Dog, please take her to Martha,* she added silently. *She loved me and my litter-brothers, and she didn't care what kind of dogs we were.*

Then Peaceful stepped forward, and Storm was deeply touched to see that she did the same, adding her own pawful of earth and "Good hunting, Tufty," even though it wasn't her own custom.

Arrow gently filled in the rest of the hole and stepped back, staring at the dark spot in the bright sunbeam. Storm joined him, nuzzling him gently, uncertain what she could say.

"That was beautiful," Peaceful said. "The Forests Beyond sound wonderful. But now it is time for me to get back to my own Pack. My absence will have been noticed."

Storm turned to her, wondering how she could possibly thank Peaceful for everything she'd done. "I hope we'll see you again," she said.

"I hope so too," said Peaceful. "Arrow . . . one last thing. I know that the pain is fresh and strong in this moment, but when you return to Bella and your litter, you should remember this day—not as the day you lost a pup, but the day you were given two."

For a moment, Arrow stiffened, and Storm thought he was holding in a huge howl of grief. Then he let it out as a long sigh and nodded. "Thank you, Peaceful. For your help, and your wisdom."

Peaceful dipped her head again, and with a last flick of her tail in Storm's direction, she turned and padded away quickly. A few long wolf-strides later, and she was gone.

CHAPTER TWELVE

Storm trotted through the trees, feeling the early light of the Sun-Dog on her back and a cool breeze stirring her fur. Many of the Sun-Dog's journeys had passed since the birth of the pups, and the weather was starting to change. There was a feeling of expectation in the air and a chill on the ground in the mornings.

The scents of prey were all around her, and she took a moment to thank the Forest-Dog for this plenty. She knew she would be able to catch enough to feed herself, Bella, and Arrow, even though Bella was still making milk to feed the pups. It was a luxury she wasn't used to, being able to pause and sample the different prey scents that crisscrossed the forest floor, working out which creatures would make the best meal.

Just another way this Pack is better than the Wild Pack, she thought. *And it is my Pack now.* Her life here had begun with both joy and tragedy, but Arrow and Bella had taken Peaceful's advice, and though they still mourned Tufty, they were focused on their living pups.

And Storm, too. Not a day went by when Bella didn't thank her for bringing Peaceful to their aid. *We only have a Pack,* she'd said, *because of you, Storm.*

She had never been in a Pack before where every Packmate, without exception, understood and loved her. Bella and Arrow had even told her she would be welcome to sleep in their den, but Storm had refused. She still, every so often, found that she had sleepwalked—usually only a few pawsteps out of the camp, but it was enough for her to be sure she didn't want to be in danger of stepping on the pups or disturbing Bella's precious sleep. She had her own den, in a small hollow that she'd dug out underneath a jutting rock, behind a wall of vines. It was cozy, and safe, and all her own. And if she ever missed the warmth and comfort of other dogs, she knew where she could find them.

Perhaps their Pack wasn't the biggest, but she was sure it was the best.

As she raised her head to sniff out the trail of a weasel she was following, a leaf dropped out of the air and tumbled across Storm's muzzle on its way to the ground. It was brown and it crunched when she nosed it.

Red Leaf was coming.

She knew it from the cooling of the air, as well as the change in the trees. It explained the abundance of prey, too—the creatures had all had a good Long Light, had grown fat and sleepy. The lean times were ahead, but Storm was confident that the Pack would be able to weather them here.

The time had passed so quickly.

Perhaps that's what happens when you're happy?

Storm arrived back in camp with two fat weasels dangling from her mouth, added them to the prey pile, and cleared a small collection of dry leaves away. The breeze carried them off, but Storm knew that it would bring more—maybe a lot more. The thin pine needles didn't seem like they would drop yet, but some of the other trees here were thickly covered in leaves as big as Storm's face, and she was a little worried that the pups would get lost underneath them if they all fell at once. . . .

Suddenly she felt something on her tail, like a small creature biting it, and she spun around.

"Scramble! No!"

The pup sat back on his haunches in shock and couldn't keep his balance—he rolled over on the ground, legs in the air and eyes wide. "No, Storm!" he giggled. "I'm *Nip*."

"Oh—sorry, Nip," Storm said. "I couldn't see your patch."

Nip giggled some more and rolled to his paws, then barked a high-pitched volley at a crunchy brown leaf that wheeled past him. "Leaf Monster!" he yapped, and he tried, and failed, to pounce on it. Storm watched him with an indulgent sigh.

It was almost impossible to tell the two pups apart. Both of them had the same fur; black like Arrow's and fluffy like Bella's. They had identical big brown eyes, identical sandy-colored paws, and even identical sandy splotches on their backs—except that Scramble's was on his left side, and Nip's was on his right.

I hope Scramble's with his Mother-Dog, she thought, *and not trying to climb a tree again.*

These pups were going to be trouble, Storm could tell. She was sure they had only opened their eyes a few days ago. They weren't even eating prey for themselves, and yet they were already running rings around their parents.

She'd thought that Lucky's pups were a handful, with Tumble's constant need to climb everything, Fluff's love of unexpectedly head-butting dogs, and Tiny's tendency to vanish and reappear somewhere Storm could have sworn she couldn't possibly reach. But Nip and Scramble were younger than those pups had been when Storm took care of them, and they were already far more mischievous.

Arrow emerged from the den with Scramble in tow. "Storm, would you watch the pups for a while?" he asked. "Bella wants to go for a run, to stretch her legs, and I'd like to go with her."

"Er—yes, that's fine," Storm said, watching as Scramble joined Nip in his hunt for the vicious Leaf Monster. Secretly she had hoped she would have time to lie down and enjoy the Red Leaf afternoon sun, without having to be on alert for escaping pups, but that was the price of being in such a small Pack—there was always something to do.

Bella emerged from the den, moving a little stiffly, but bright-eyed. She trotted over to Storm and gave her an affectionate lick on the end of her nose.

"Thank you, Storm. Be good for Storm, pups!" she told her litter, but they were too busy trying to climb a small rock at the edge of the camp. Bella rolled her eyes happily, and she and Arrow headed out into the trees.

Storm moved closer to the pups, since she might have to catch one if it fell—

But she was too late. Scramble had already reached the top of the rock, yipped with triumph, and bounced on all four paws—and somehow lost his balance and tumbled off into the grass. Storm started forward to check that he was all right, but Scramble was already up and glaring at his litter-brother.

"Nip push!" he barked.

"Not me," Nip replied, sitting back on his haunches with a thump.

"Now, Scramble," Storm said, leaning down to give the pup a lick on the top of his head. "Are you listening? Listen to me. Nip was on the ground, wasn't he?"

"Yes," muttered Scramble, after a long pause for thought.

"So he couldn't have pushed you off the rock, could he?"

"No."

"Was *Tufty*," yipped Nip.

Storm felt her ears drooping slightly.

Not this again . . .

She wasn't sure it was a good idea for Bella have told them about Tufty so soon. Of course, Storm understood the urge to make sure that poor Tufty was remembered by her litter-brothers, but they were still so small. They couldn't possibly understand about life and death at their age, so if they were told they had a litter-sister, one who had to go away, what were they supposed to think?

Except that they hadn't asked where she went. That was the strange part—the two pups had decided, seemingly all by themselves, that Tufty was *still here*. The adult dogs just couldn't *see* her.

Bella and Arrow corrected them when they heard this and told Storm that all pups had strange imaginations, and they would grow out of it. But it worried Storm. She'd been a pup much more recently than either of them, and she didn't remember playing anything like this with her litter-brothers.

She watched as the two pups gamboled across the clearing, playing with the leaf. Nip biffed it with a paw, passing it to Scramble, who jumped on it and bit it, then patted it away—to nobody. It lay twitching in the grass for a moment, with neither of the two pups trying to catch it. They both just sat and watched the empty space. Then the wind pulled it up and Nip went after it again.

It's like there is *a third pup in their game,* Storm thought, with a shudder. *They're imagining that their sister is still alive to play with them. It's almost as if they* can *see her.*

It made Storm's fur prickle to think about it.

Storm stepped into the space between Lucky and Mickey, and she felt at once that she was home. She wasn't sure why she had stayed away so long. Every dog in the Pack was looking at her with love. She forgave them all for the way they had treated her—they had made it right, and now she knew this was where she should be.

The dogs lifted their muzzles to the sky, and Storm did the same. The moon was huge, and so close she could almost make out the faint shapes of wolves moving on its surface. Or perhaps she was imagining it.

As one, the Pack began the Great Howl, and Storm had never felt so perfectly connected to them before. She could feel them breathing as she breathed, and see the Spirit Dogs walking among them, faint presences stopping to nuzzle or speak to the other dogs, one by one.

Then . . . it came. Every pawstep sounding out, quiet, as if it was walking over hardstone instead of grass. Storm couldn't turn to look at it, but she felt its presence, its malevolence. When it passed by the other dogs, their eyes widened and their ears went back, and then they turned their gazes on Storm. One by one, the light of love went out, replaced by the gleam of suspicion. Lucky, Daisy, Moon, even Sunshine—when the Fear-Dog passed them, they shuddered and turned on one another. On Storm.

There was something else, too. A dog. Was it the same one that had she had once dreamed watched her from the forest shadows? It was sitting in the middle of the circle of dogs, in the heart of the Pack, watching the Fear-Dog's progress.

"Is the Fear-Dog your master," Storm asked, "or are you his?"

The strange dog did not reply. It only opened its jaws and let out a sound like pebbles rolling down a slope—a rattling sound that made Storm leap to her paws. Her Pack was in danger! She growled . . .

. . . and she was still growling as her eyes snapped open and she stared around, jolted awake. She was on her paws, in the camp, outside her den. The Moon-Dog's light was so bright she almost thought it was the Sun-Dog, until her eyes properly adjusted.

Something's wrong. There's danger here.

The hissing, rattling noise was still going.

Storm's hackles rose and she growled again. She blinked the sleep out of her eyes and shook herself, trying to focus. There was danger. She could sense it, and *hear* it, but not see it!

Then she spotted something—a red leaf moving, and then a few blades of grass. She stepped closer, and now she could see a long body in pale and dark brown, slithering across the grass toward Bella's den, shaking its tail, which was making that weird rattling hiss. Two keen, beady black eyes shone on its pointy head, trained on the entrance.

A snake! And it was heading straight for the pups.

"Get away!" Storm barked, though the thing didn't seem to have ears. She leaped toward it, her heart pounding. She had seen a snake before, but never hunted or fought one—how did you catch such a strange, quick, wriggling thing?

The snake paused, and its head snapped around to face Storm. It opened its jaws, farther even than any dog Storm had ever met, revealing gleaming, deadly-looking white fangs.

They carry poison in their teeth, Twitch had told her once. He'd told her to stay away.

Well, I can't! It'll hurt the pups!

The snake hissed again and rattled its lumpy tail, and Storm fought the urge to back off.

There was only one thing for it. The thing had no legs, no way to fight back, if you didn't count those sharp, poisonous teeth and the speed it could move its head. . . .

She feinted to her left, the snake lunged, and Storm twisted and pushed off, coming around to her right instead, fangs at the ready. She grabbed the snake between her teeth, right behind its head. The body flailed, the tail smacking against her chest and neck, but she had the creature where she wanted it. With a flick of her head, she tossed the snake as far away from the den as she could. It landed upside down in the grass and immediately started wriggling to right itself.

There was a scrambling behind her and Arrow came out of

the den, panting, looking around as if he had just been startled awake too. He saw the snake, and his pant turned into a growl. He ran to Storm's side and they both flung a volley of furious barking at the snake. Having righted itself, it slithered quickly away into the bushes. Storm took a few steps forward, still barking, until she was certain that the snake was not coming back.

She turned back to find Bella and the pups watching her, as well as Arrow. They were sitting in the mouth of the den, and for once Nip and Scramble were perfectly quiet, their eyes huge and wide. They seemed frightened, and when Storm walked toward them, Nip's legs trembled.

"Thank you, Storm!" Bella yapped. "You saved us! Say thank you, pups."

"Thank Storm," Nip whined, and his legs stopped shaking. "Storm did a big bark!"

"*Loud*," said Scramble.

"Yes, it was," said Arrow. "Thank goodness you were awake, Storm."

"Actually," Storm said, "I—I wasn't. Not at first. I was having a dream. I thought I was back in the Wild Pack, but they were in danger—there was a dog making a noise just like the snake. I tried to protect them, but then I woke up, and I was already on my paws. I . . . was growling at the snake in my sleep."

She hung her head. She was prepared for Bella to draw back, for Arrow to step between her and the pups. But they didn't.

"That's quite some nose for danger you have," said Bella. "You must have sensed the snake, and somehow it got into your dream. You were trying to save us, even though you didn't know what from." She nosed at the pups. "Come on, it isn't awake time for little dogs yet. Back to the den with you."

Scramble stared at Storm for a moment longer, his eyes thoughtful. "Loud bark," he said. "Big, loud bark!"

"A big, *big* bark," Nip agreed. Bella huffed into their fur and nudged them inside, and they went without complaining.

"Do you think you can get back to sleep?" Arrow asked Storm. She sighed.

"Maybe in a little while," she said. "Not now." Her heart was beating too fast—and the memory of the Wild Pack's peace being broken by the mysterious dog in her dream was a little too fresh.

"I don't feel sleepy either," said Arrow. "Let's just sit with the Moon-Dog for a bit."

Storm sat down in the middle of the clearing, relieved and grateful for the company. Arrow sat beside her, and for a moment they fell into a comfortable silence.

It was a nice dream, until the Fear-Dog came, Storm thought.

It had been wonderful to see her old Pack again, to know that they wanted her there, and all their old arguments had been settled. Was that possible? Being here, with Arrow, Bella, and the pups, had shown her what it was like to be in a Pack that accepted her. It was all she had ever wanted, but Storm had to admit that a small part of her still wished that the acceptance could have come from the Wild Pack instead.

She suddenly glanced at Arrow and realized that she had never really told him, or Bella, about what had made her leave the Wild Pack. They hadn't asked—perhaps they thought it was none of their business, or that she would talk if she wanted to.

"Arrow," she murmured, "can I ask you something?"

"Of course," he said, lying down on his side in the grass, sniffing at a passing beetle.

"Do you ever regret leaving the Pack? The Wild Pack?"

"Ha!" Arrow let out an amused bark, then cringed, glancing at the den where Bella was presumably trying to get the two pups back to sleep. "No, Storm, I don't. Not that Bella and I had much of a choice," he added, and his voice was quiet but it was angry. "It was made perfectly clear that we had no place there. I'm much happier with just us. I don't need to scrape and whine for acceptance, just because I was born into Blade's Pack. I betrayed *her* to save *their* necks, that Ice Wind, and yet they treated me like I was going to turn into her at any moment. There were plenty of dogs in your old Pack I didn't like one bit anyway, and I certainly don't miss them."

Storm huffed a heavy breath through her teeth. His candid opinion chimed with hers so closely, and yet, for all their prejudice and stupidity, she *liked* most of the Wild Pack. Or she had.

"Which dogs didn't you like?" she asked, curiosity getting the better of her.

"Let me think," Arrow said drily. "I certainly don't miss Chase picking her fleas all the time, or Mickey drooling in his sleep and making the bedding damp."

Storm cocked her head to one side. Those were annoying habits, she had to admit—but when she thought of Mickey's lolling tongue getting stuck to the moss, or Chase trying to scratch the back of her own head on a tree trunk, all she really felt was a rush of fondness for her old Packmates.

"I can see your point," she said. "But you have to admit, those are pretty small complaints. They're good dogs, at heart."

"Hmm," said Arrow. "Most of them, yes. Most of them were just weak."

Storm stared at him, and he shook his head.

"You know it's true. Take Sweet and Lucky, for instance. They talked a big talk about protecting their Pack and their pups, but they were weak and scared. They said they loved you, and . . . well, I don't doubt they did. But they never stood up to help you when the others turned against you. I don't talk about this with Bella," he added, lowering his voice even more. "He's her litter-brother. She doesn't want to think about how much he failed us."

Storm felt as if she was trying to walk into a strong wind—Arrow's feelings were so like her own, and so not like them, all at the same time. She didn't know whether to wag her tail or let it droop.

"I can admit that Sweet and Lucky were *trying* to be good Packmates, but they failed," Arrow went on. "I can't be so kind about some of the others. Breeze, for example."

"Really?" Storm said, cocking one ear curiously. "You don't think Breeze was trying to be a good Packmate?"

"Humph. I don't know about that. All I know is, she was a cruel and sneaky dog, and I wouldn't have her in my Pack for all the fish in the lake."

"*Cruel?*" Storm repeated. She thought about Breeze, wondering if Arrow had somehow gotten her mixed up with some other dog. She supposed his comments about Lucky and Sweet hadn't come as a big surprise, but he seemed to be saying that Breeze was actually a bad dog.

"Oh yes. I was surprised that Sweet and Lucky let her spend so much time with their pups—but of course, they probably didn't know. I had a bad feeling about her while I was in the Pack, but it wasn't until after we'd left that I learned she used to go on hunts and bring back prey just for herself."

Storm recoiled, shocked. "No! But—Breeze wasn't even a hunt dog, she was a scout!"

"Well, perhaps she didn't make a habit of it. I only saw her do it once. But believe me, I know what I saw. It was after we'd left the Pack, but not the territory. I was hunting, and I saw Breeze with my own eyes, heading back in the direction of the camp all by herself, with a rabbit in her jaws. And she hadn't even killed it. The poor creature was struggling, in pain. She should have snapped its neck, but she was just letting it suffer while she slunk through the bushes, making sure no dog saw her. Like I said: cruel."

Storm sat back on her haunches, staring up at the Moon-Dog.

Breeze . . . cruel and sneaky?

She couldn't believe it—it didn't match at all with the sweet-natured, helpful dog that Storm thought she knew. But at the

177

same time, she was certain that Arrow wouldn't lie to her. And it was unlikely he could have been mistaken, either—he was sharp-eyed and he would know what he saw.

But if it's true . . . what else didn't I know about my Packmates?

CHAPTER THIRTEEN

Storm padded along the edge of the stream, her senses on high alert for any scent or sound of prey moving near the water. Everything needed water, she reasoned, and she could do with finding some bigger prey—the pups would be weaned soon, and they seemed to have bottomless appetites.

She felt refreshed from the extra sleep she'd had that morning after she and Arrow had drifted off in the middle of the clearing.

She tried not to think too much about the Wild Pack. After all, their problems were no longer her problems. She had plenty of her own—like hunting down a meal for three adult dogs and two pups just starting to eat prey, patrolling a territory, pup-sitting, and now apparently keeping out snakes too. She couldn't dwell on anything Arrow had said.

Luckily, before she could begin to dwell on it anyway, she

caught a strong scent of rabbit around the edge of the stream. If she could catch a nice fat rabbit or two, that would go a long way toward feeding her Pack. She followed the scent, leaving the stream, and soon found herself at the top of a small, sloping meadow. It was exactly the kind of place where rabbits loved to nest—but she knew if they had dug their dens deep into the hillside, she would never be able to dig them out all by herself. The only way to catch one of these rabbits was going to be by stealth. She made sure that the wind wasn't carrying her scent across the meadow, and then lowered her belly to the ground and shuffled carefully forward.

Slowly, taking the greatest care not to make any sudden movements, she raised her head until she could peer over the tops of the long blades of grass.

Yes. There were several rabbits outside their dens, lolloping around the meadow, and they seemed totally unaware of Storm's presence. She narrowed her eyes, and soon she had picked out a nice big one. It moved slowly, one hop at a time, stopping frequently to eat the grass and stare at the sky with slightly bulging eyes.

Storm didn't move. She settled down to wait. If she sprang too soon, they would outpace her and be deep in their dens before she could catch one. If she waited too long, one of them might scent her there, and the same thing would happen.

Come a little closer, she goaded the nice fat rabbit. *Come on, over here . . . tasty grass here. . . .*

Almost as if it'd heard her, the rabbit turned in Storm's direction. She bunched her muscles, ready to spring, and held her breath, and then . . .

She was on the rabbit, her teeth in its neck, before it had time to react. The other rabbits thumped across the meadow and dived into their dens, but Storm didn't care. She killed the rabbit with a hard shake that broke its spine cleanly and, Storm thought, probably almost painlessly.

. . . she hadn't even killed it. The poor creature was struggling, in pain . . .

Arrow's voice echoed in Storm's head as she looked down at the prey creature.

There was nothing wrong with killing for food, of course. And there was nothing wrong with enjoying the hunt, either. But that was just it—there was satisfaction in well-caught prey, in the heart-pounding chase but also in the quick, clean kill.

Not in *suffering.*

Storm picked up the limp rabbit in her jaws and turned away from the meadow. There would be no more rabbits to catch there today, but in a day or two, perhaps.

A flurry of wind filled her nose with scents from the opposite bank of the stream. As she breathed in the now-familiar musk of wolf, she realized she must be closer to their territory than she had thought. She knew that she ought to take the prey straight back to camp, but as she walked along the bank of the cool stream, she found herself looking across it, thinking of Peaceful and Thoughtful.

She hadn't seen any of the wolves since the pups were born. That was probably a good thing. She certainly didn't want to run into any of the wolves that had caught her last time. But when she thought about Nip and Scramble, playing happily and sleeping curled up with their parent-dogs, she was flooded with a desire to find the two wolves that had helped them so much. She would like to talk to them again.

Storm cast around for somewhere safe to leave the rabbit and found a hollow tree, perhaps where a bird had nested once, though it smelled as if the bird was long gone. She left her prey in the hollow, hoping that the strange hiding spot would keep it away from any other hunters that came along, and gingerly crossed the shallow stream.

The Sky-Dogs had had a brief tussle the previous day, and

there had been a short squall that left some muddy ground around the streambed, dotted with leaves that were starting to break up and decay.

Excellent. Storm lay down and rolled in the mud and leaves, taking a puppyish delight in how thoroughly she could cover herself. Far more delight than she had felt when Mickey first taught her this trick to disguise her scent, back when she actually *was* a pup.

When she thought she might smell more of earth than of dog, she slipped through the trees and onto the wolf Pack's territory.

She moved carefully, one pawstep at a time, remembering the way the wolves had come upon her out of nowhere. The scratch on her back was healed, but she felt it itching as she remembered the Wolf Alpha's claws coming down.

Then again, it had been dark, and she had run into the middle of their territory howling at the top of her lungs for help. She liked to think that if she was trying not to be caught, she would have a much better chance. Besides, even if she was, Thoughtful had said she had one warning left. She didn't want another scratch, but she could think of worse things.

She followed a scent line that seemed to form a sort of boundary—perhaps the official edge of the territory, according to the wolves—around through the trees to her right, and then up a rocky slope. Thinking of the shape of the valley, she guessed that she would come out on the longpaw-made cliff. And sure enough, she climbed and climbed, and then pushed through between two bushes and found herself on a small ledge, high above the small, still lake and the wolf Pack's camp.

It seemed as if she had come just in time to witness some sort of gathering. The camp was full of wolves—so *many* of them, it was incredible to watch—some of them lounging in the sun, others lying in small groups, grooming or playing with one another, or dipping their long muzzles into the cool lake.

Storm kept her head low, as far back from the edge as she could go without losing her view. Slowly, the wolves began to converge on the center of the camp, forming a ring around one wolf. At first, Storm assumed this was the Alpha, but this wolf didn't seem as imposing.

It's Peaceful! Storm realized, with a sharp stab of anxiety. She told herself to stay calm—after all, a Healer must have plenty of cause to address their Pack.

But then the Wolf Alpha stepped forward out of the ring and turned slowly, addressing the Pack in a growl that rang out clearly up on Storm's ledge.

"It is Full Moon," she said. "And we have howled to our ancestors for the past two nights. Today I bring Peaceful, our Healer, before you to invoke Full Truth. Peaceful," she turned to the Healer, who stood tall and proud and still under the gazes of her Packmates. "You understand that under the Full Moon, you are bound to tell the truth?"

Bound? How? Storm wondered, her stomach dropping even more.

"Yes, Alpha," said Peaceful in a clear voice.

"Then let us once and for all get to the bottom of this matter. Peaceful: under the Full Moon, in front of your Pack, do you deny that you helped that raggedy band of dogs that lives just beyond our borders, dares to call itself a Pack, and harbors a mutt who has repeatedly violated our territory?"

"No, Alpha," said Peaceful. "I do not deny it."

A howl of anger and shock went up from the wolves. It seemed to get right under Storm's skin. She searched the wolf faces for Thoughtful and found him—not howling, but whining, his head hanging low.

"This is a crime of four parts," snarled the Alpha, and Storm shuddered. What was that Thoughtful had told her about four things? That she should hope she never got to the fourth warning?

185

"You spoke secretly to a dog. You assisted a dog. You acknowledged dog territory, and you lied to your Pack. Did you do these things?"

Just tell them no! Storm willed Peaceful. *How can the Full Moon force you to tell the truth? That doesn't make any sense!*

But she already knew the gentle Healer wolf too well to believe that she would lie.

Peaceful's stance still didn't give away any fear, but this time there was a tremble in her voice as she spoke.

"I did, Alpha."

More howls and mutterings from the other wolves, and now some of them were snarling and snapping their jaws at Peaceful.

"Traitor!" one of the wolves barked.

"She nurtures our enemies!" said another one, a Mother-Wolf with a litter of large cubs around her feet.

Storm's fur prickled and her heart ached with the familiarity of it. She knew what it was like, to have done what was right and be punished for it. She remembered the pregnant fox she had spared from being wounded. The wolves obviously thought themselves superior to dogs, the same way dogs did to foxes.

Peaceful raised her head high.

"I did these things, and I stand by them. I entered the dog

camp to help one of them get through a birth that would have killed her and all her pups. Whether we like it or not, dogs are our distant kin. I could not stand by and watch an innocent dog, who has done nothing to me, suffer and die so horribly. Her pups are not so different from your cubs, Careful," she added. "And I would never let cubs die if I could prevent it."

This was obviously the wrong thing to say. The Mother-Wolf, Careful, looked a little less bloodthirsty, and so did a small handful of others—but the rest of them only bayed louder.

"Compare us to dogs?" one of the wolves howled. "Are you mad?"

"How dare you!" another growled. "Take that back!"

They really hate *dogs,* Storm thought. *And yet, clearly not all of them . . .*

"QUIET!" the Wolf Alpha howled, and at once a cold silence fell across the valley. Storm thought even the birds had stopped singing. "Peaceful is one of our own, and we take care of our own. But we do not tolerate betrayal, either. My command is that Peaceful will be exiled from the Pack for two days. She must leave our territory and not reenter it until High Sun on the third day."

Storm saw Thoughtful's ears droop sadly. She was puzzled— exile for two days hardly seemed like much punishment at all! It was not enough time to get truly hungry, or even lonely.

After all, I should know. I had no choice but to go into exile.

"When you return," the Alpha went on, turning to Peaceful, "you will be given the chance to apologize. If you are still unrepentant, other punishments will be in store. Now, go."

Peaceful started walking, and the ring of wolves opened up to let her pass. The Alpha sat back on her haunches and watched, as the closest wolves snapped their teeth at Peaceful, and barked, and began to follow her. Without looking back, Peaceful broke into a run, with the snapping jaws and angry barking of her own Pack at her heels. Even Thoughtful was there, running along at the back of the group, not snarling at his litter-sister but seeming to go along with the Pack's wishes.

Storm looked on with horror and guilt, pressing her belly to the stone.

I need to get out of here. Thoughtful's right—I really don't want to find out what happens to a dog after the fourth warning.

She turned and hurried down the rocky slope, as fast as she could go without tripping or sending loose stones rattling ahead of her. She made it to the stream without hearing the heavy tread of wolf pawsteps or any more howls of fury. The rabbit was still where she had left it, and she pulled it out of its hollow tree stump and began to walk, slowly, back to the camp.

There were five mouths to feed back at the camp, and she knew it was the right thing to do. But all the way, Peaceful's gentle voice speaking up for her, for Bella, echoed in her mind. After all, she was right. As different as they might be, dogs and wolves were distant kin. And without her help, Bella, Nip, and Scramble would all have died along with poor Tufty.

When she reached the camp, Storm had made up her mind.

It's time I repaid Peaceful for her kindness.

CHAPTER FOURTEEN

Storm lay on her belly in the grass at the edge of the rabbit meadow, watching them intently. She hadn't intended to come back so soon, but then her plans had changed.

It seemed that she had caught the biggest, least observant rabbit in the meadow yesterday. She lay in the grass for what felt like a frustratingly long time. Prey passed by, some of them so close Storm could almost have snapped them up without moving—but she held herself back, knowing that if she missed, they would go to ground and the hunt would be over. She waited, letting her scent mingle with the grass, until finally two smaller rabbits hopped toward her.

Two small rabbits will do, she thought, *instead of one big one.*

She waited and waited, until finally they were almost right on top of her nose, and then she sprang, seizing one rabbit in her jaws and smacking the other to the ground with her paws. It was a neat kill, and she left the meadow with the prey swinging from her mouth, feeling warm and smug.

She began to zigzag across the land, staying carefully outside the wolves' territory but venturing near it and then away again. The delicious scent of the fresh prey was distracting, but she focused hard on anything that *wasn't* tasty rabbit. She made her way downhill, until the land flattened a little and she thought she was level with the bottom of the wolf Pack's valley—and sure enough, just outside their territory, she picked up the scent of a lone wolf and hurried toward it.

She found Peaceful the Healer wolf dozing under the shade of a tree, her tail curled around her back paws and her muzzle laid flat on the crunchy red leaves.

"Hello, Peaceful," Storm barked, dropping the rabbits at her paws. "I'm so glad I found you!"

Peaceful sat up, blinking in surprise. She stared for a moment at Storm and at the rabbits by her paws, and then her ears flattened to her skull and she backed away. "Don't come any closer."

"Peaceful?" Storm whined. "What's wrong? It's just me. I know you were exiled from your Pack. I just want to help."

The wolf's tail dropped between her legs and she hung her

head. "Oh, Storm. You can't do that."

What did those other wolves do to you? Storm wondered. *Why are you so frightened of me? I'm only about half your size.*

She lay down her belly, making herself even smaller, and nudged the rabbits toward Peaceful with her nose. "I know how hard it can be to hunt alone," she said. "And we owe you so much—Bella and the pups are doing so well now, and if it hadn't been for you—"

"Storm, please stop. That's exactly why you need to leave." Peaceful shook herself and sat down. "It's so kind of you, but I can't accept this prey, and I can't let you come any closer. I return to my Pack in two days, and if they smell your scent on me, I'll be in even *more* trouble. They'll ask if I've been talking to dogs, and I cannot lie to my Pack. Do you understand?"

Storm wasn't sure that she did.

"But you didn't seek me out, I found you," she said. "How can they blame you if I *decide* to bring you something to eat? And who cares what they think anyway?" she added, with a low growl.

"I do," Peaceful said gently. "They're my Pack. I can't leave them, so I must live by their rules."

"But their rules are foolish, if they punish you for showing kindness to creatures who need you. Dogs and wolves are so alike. . . ."

Peaceful huffed and shook her head. "Don't let any other wolf hear you say so! It's one of the oldest rules of the wolf Pack. We believe that wolves are the first creation of the Great Wolf who made the whole world, and the most important. We don't *lower* ourselves to ally with any other creature, *especially* not dogs. Some-times," she added, looking around as if she was afraid she might be overheard, "I think that rule was made because dogs *are* so much like us. To keep us thinking we're better. We might not be able to look down on dogs so comfortably if we spent more time with them."

"I knew a dog who was half wolf, once," Storm said. "If all wolves believe that dogs are so far below them, then . . ."

Peaceful's eyes went wide. "His Mother- or Father-Wolf must have been very brave, or very stupid, to mate with a dog."

Which were *Alpha's parents?* Storm wondered. *Were they brave or stupid? Perhaps they were a little of both.*

"I wish I could accept the help and friendship you're offering, Storm," said Peaceful. "But I cannot antagonize Alpha any more. I've already been shown mercy."

"You have?" Storm whined. "But they seemed so angry."

"Most of my kind consider dogs our enemy. To them, I am the worst sort of traitor. But two days is not very long," Peaceful

193

panted, relaxing a little and scratching behind her ear with one of her huge, powerful back paws. "I was given a light punishment, because I am the Healer wolf and they don't want me to be away long, not really. I must respect that and not make things worse, for me or my Pack."

"I understand," said Storm. She pawed at one of the rabbits. "I suppose I should go, then. And . . . I'll take my one rabbit with me. The *one rabbit* I brought here."

Peaceful's ears twitched with amusement.

"You are funny, Storm. Take both rabbits—the pups need them more than I do. But thank you again. I wish you and your Pack good hunting, and the blessings of the Great Wolf."

Storm bowed her head. "And may the Spirit Dogs watch over you too, Peaceful."

She picked up both rabbits and turned away.

Even though Peaceful hadn't seemed too sad to send her away, Storm felt a gloom descend over her as she walked.

Peaceful had done nothing any rational dog or wolf could call *wrong*. It was only the wolves' strange beliefs that had forced them to punish her.

The echo of her own exile from the Wild Pack stung, as if she was walking through thorns.

Peaceful is a good wolf, and I'm a good dog, she thought. *I may not always have followed the rules, but all I ever wanted to do was keep the Pack safe. Sweet and Lucky should have understood that.*

So why didn't they?

The Spirit Dogs had shown no sign that they distrusted Storm or thought her a bad dog, so why would the dogs in her Pack? They weren't stupid dogs, not really, but something kept on making them push her away. Whenever she thought she was earning their trust, something would happen or some dog would say something about Fierce Dogs and she would find herself under suspicion again. . . .

Could it possibly have been a coincidence? That when some dog tried to defend her, they always somehow made it worse? Breeze's voice echoed in her mind, and there was a sly tone in it that Storm hadn't noticed before. She wondered if she was imagining it.

Not Storm . . . she's not like those other Fierce Dogs . . . she's big and strong but she wouldn't hurt us. . . .

Maybe Breeze hadn't said those exact words, not all together, but she'd said things like them, and the effect had always been to make the rest of the Pack *more* suspicious, not less.

Storm's fur bristled, the way it did when she was out on a hunt, or a patrol, and thought she could sense a . . . *presence*. She knew that there was a reason she was remembering this, but she could not put her paw on what it was.

Why am I remembering Breeze sticking up for me? she wondered. *Because there was something strange . . . not about* what *she said, but* how *she—*

A furious howl split the air around Storm, and her ears pressed to her skull as she looked around to see wolves—three of them, approaching her at the speed of the Wind-Dogs.

"There she is!" one of them barked.

Storm knew she should run, but her legs were stiff with panic, and she hadn't been paying attention to where she was walking, her head too full of betrayal and confusion to heed what her nose was telling her. She was back on the wolves' territory again. She turned clumsily on the spot—she had to get out, but which was the way back to her own camp?

Spirit Dogs, where am I?

And then there were two more wolves melting out of the shadows of the trees, and one of them was the giant Alpha, her long fangs bared in an angry snarl.

"Are you so stupid, dog? Do you not understand me when I tell you this is our territory? Answer!"

"I understand," Storm growled, almost involuntarily, dropping her rabbits at her paws. "I made a mistake, that's all."

"You certainly did. The Still-Water Pack does not suffer dogs to stroll through our territory whenever they please." She raised her head and howled. "Bright, give this dog her third warning."

Storm saw an opening between two of the wolves and tried to dart between them, but one of them raised her huge paws and brought them down on Storm's flank, knocking her off-balance. "Not so fast, *dog*," she barked, baring her teeth, about to snap at Storm's foreleg. Storm twisted, raking her claws through the wolf's thick fur. She didn't think she'd hurt her—the wolf yelped, but with surprise, not pain—but it was enough of a distraction to wriggle up and out of her grip.

Then the other three wolves piled in.

Teeth closed over Storm's tail. She yelped and snapped at the closest wolf, a red mist of fury starting to creep around the edges of her vision. She found herself tearing at a mouthful of fur, tasting blood. The wolf howled and swiped at Storm's muzzle, but she held on tight. The teeth in her tail let go and so did she. She spun, snapping at the wolves in turn, making herself a moving, biting target.

Again, she felt the smack of huge paws on her side and almost went down, but this time she writhed and skittered away, kicking up a small shower of crunching leaves.

Wherever she turned, there were at least two wolves she couldn't see. She felt claws catch in the skin on her back but shook them off and turned, fast, and managed to seize the wolf's ear between her teeth. It tore, and the wolf cringed back with a whimper of pain before lunging forward again and head-butting Storm in the chest. Storm tumbled backward as the great thump knocked the air out of her. She landed on her back, right under a wolf's muzzle. She scrambled to her paws again, wincing as the wounds on her back stretched and rubbed across the ground. Her chest ached, and her tail stung, but she was alive.

They can't be trying to kill me, she thought. *He could have torn my throat out.*

Now the wolves were circling her, growling but wary, and she forced herself to growl and snap at them again, even though breathing was hard and she was starting to tire.

They're not used to prey that bites back! she thought.

The wolves were so comfortable in their valley, with no real enemies, they weren't expecting her to put up any kind of fight. But even so, how long would they keep this up? She could feel the blood running down her tail, and as she tried to dodge another snap, her back leg gave way underneath her and she sprawled in the red leaves. She staggered back up, her breath rasping in her throat. One of the wolves lunged to her left and she dodged away—too late, she saw the wolf's paw coming in on her right, felt its claws connect with the side of her muzzle. She tumbled back to the ground, hot blood running down the side of her face, afraid to open her eye.

Get up. Get. Up.

She started to feel panic bubbling in her stomach. Had she been foolish to believe in the promise of three warnings? This was starting to feel like much more than a warning. After all, how could she be sure that wolves always did what they said? Her legs were shaking, but she pulled herself to her paws. Another wolf paw slammed down toward her, and she reared back and caught the leg in her jaws instead, but her grip was loose and the wolf tore free easily. She stumbled and then crashed to the ground with the full weight of one of the wolves on her back, its claws ready to rake through her fur. She wriggled desperately, but—

"That's enough," said the Alpha. The wolf on Storm's back didn't move. "Errant, *enough*," the Alpha growled, so low Storm could almost feel it like a Growl of the Earth-Dog underneath her skin.

The weight lifted. Storm tried to get up, but the Alpha's huge paw came down on top of her splayed leg.

"This was your third and final warning. If you trespass here again, the fourth will be a warning for all your kind." The Alpha lowered her muzzle so Storm could feel the huge wolf's breath hot on her face. "Let me say this so that a dog can understand: if we see you here again, we will kill you."

She stood back, and all the wolves turned and began to walk away from Storm. She didn't try to get up. Out of the corner of her eye, she saw the wolf who the Alpha had called Bright pause and lower her muzzle to the grass, sniffing. Then she raised her head, and Storm saw she had picked up Storm's prey, the two rabbits, and she trotted after her Alpha with them dangling from her jaws.

Storm was too tired to feel angry. Instead she lay on her belly, watched the wolves and her catch disappear into the valley, and waited for her strength to return.

CHAPTER FIFTEEN

Storm limped down the slope into camp, every stumbling step feeling like there were heavy rocks attached to her paws. Her tail hurt when it swung, and it hurt even more when she tried to keep it still. She was desperate to lie down and lick the wounds on her back, but she couldn't reach.

Two small dark shapes tumbled over and over in the dry leaves. Storm was happy to see the pups, but guilt pinched her insides too—she'd intended to hunt for them, even if Peaceful had taken the rabbits from her. Now she had nothing, and she would be a burden on the Pack, all because of her own foolishness. . . .

"Storm! Storm!" yipped Scramble, sitting up on his haunches so fast he lost his balance and tumbled over onto his back.

Nip looked up, his tongue hanging out, but then shrank back with a whimper, and his eyes grew huge and dark.

"Storm hurt!" he yelped. "Mother-Dog!"

Scramble took a few steps toward Storm, then shuffled sideways awkwardly, as if he wanted to come closer but his paws wouldn't let him.

Storm sank down into the leaf-strewn grass. "I'm all right, pups," she said, as reassuringly as she could. "Everything's okay."

Bella emerged from the den and scrambled over to Storm, her ears pinned back. "Storm! What happened to you?"

Storm swallowed, her throat still feeling raw. She glanced at the pups.

What can I say? I don't want to frighten them.

Bella seemed to understand. She turned to the pups and licked them both on their small, soft heads. "You two go inside the den. Storm's fine, but you need to get comfy in the new bedding I put down, don't you?"

Nip nodded silently, his eyes still wide and fixed on Storm's wounds.

"Go on, then."

The two pups slowly padded inside the den, and soon Storm heard them yapping and tumbling as their game started up again.

"Now what *happened*?" Bella said, sitting down beside Storm and starting to gently lick her wounds. Storm winced as the open scratches along her back moved under Bella's tongue.

"I was . . . distracted, on my way back from hunting. I drifted onto wolf territory. They—they know that Peaceful helped us, and they weren't happy about it."

"Oh, *Storm*," Bella muttered into her fur.

"It was my own fault. I didn't mean to end up back there, but I wasn't looking where I was going. The Alpha wouldn't listen to me. She made her wolves attack me . . . they kept pushing me back, clawing me . . . one of them bit my tail," she whimpered. "I could tell they weren't going to kill me, but they were so much bigger and stronger, it felt like they could keep going forever. Then the Alpha called them off, and they let me go. But they took the rabbits I'd caught."

"So all this was just a warning?" Bella asked.

"The third warning," said Storm. "Thoughtful told me that the wolves think in fours: this time it was a warning, but next time they see me, or maybe any of us . . ."

Bella hesitated in her grooming, and Storm sighed and dropped her muzzle onto her paws.

"I'm sorry, Bella. I never meant to put any of you in danger. And the pups . . ." Storm squeezed her eyes shut. If this was the Wild Pack, she would be facing more punishment, maybe High

Watch or demotion to Patrol Dog, and Lucky would be looking at her with that floppy-eared expression that said, *What are we going to do with you, Storm?*

"Well it's not *your* fault," huffed Bella. Storm opened her eyes and turned to look at the golden dog, but one of the wounds across her shoulders pulled painfully and she winced and faced forward again. "It's those wolves who are being unreasonable," Bella went on. "You shouldn't have been on their territory, but you only went there before because you needed help. There's no need for this. We'll be careful, Storm, don't worry. We'll hunt in the other direction, keep to the uphill slope. And once the pups are old enough we'll move camp, farther from the wolves. Then they won't have any reason to hurt us."

Storm let out a breath as a long whine. "Thanks, Bella."

Bella laid her muzzle down across Storm's back, a warm and gentle pressure. "Are you all right, Storm? It's not like you not to be on your guard."

"I was a little distracted," Storm admitted. "I—well, I met Peaceful. She's been exiled from her Pack for two days for helping us."

Bella gave an angry *ruff!* "Those wolves! They don't know what they have in a wolf like Peaceful. They don't deserve her."

"That's what I thought," Storm said. "I tried to help her, but she said she had to be loyal to her Pack—even though they called her a bad wolf, when she's not! It . . . it got me thinking about our Pack. I mean the Wild Pack. They all thought I was a bad dog. . . ."

"But you're not." Bella nodded. "You're a good dog. All you ever did was try to help and protect them, and they never gave you a chance, not really."

Storm whined. "It's strange, though. If anything, it was trying to help that always seemed to get me in trouble! I wanted to find the bad dog so badly I couldn't stop poking around. I was always in the wrong place at the wrong time, somehow. It was as if some dog was always telling them not to trust me." She was about to mention her new thoughts about Breeze before closing her jaws again. Somehow, she was nervous about saying it out loud. The Wild Pack being menaced by a formless bad dog was somehow less scary than believing her former Packmate was behind all the trouble.

"They just couldn't let go of their fear of Fierce Dogs," muttered Bella. "If they couldn't see the real Storm, that's their loss. Look at what happened with that snake. You sensed danger and responded before you had even woken up. Even in your sleep, you protected the pups of your Pack!"

A strange prickling feeling ran down Storm's back that had nothing to do with the wounds the wolves had inflicted on her. A memory was coming back to her—a vision of darkness, the smell of salt, and the Fear-Dog pacing behind her.

"In my sleep . . . I sensed danger," Storm whispered. "That's *right*. I thought I was losing my mind—why would I take Tumble from the Pack down to the lakeshore? I knew I meant him no harm, but I couldn't explain why I did it."

She looked up and realized that Bella had sat up on her haunches and was staring at her, her head cocked to one side.

"That was the reason I had to leave the Wild Pack," Storm explained, getting up stiffly. "In my sleep, I took Tumble down to the lake and told him to hide there, in a cave. Tumble didn't know why I did it, and I couldn't remember, but now I know I was dreaming about the Fear-Dog."

She shook herself, even though it made her wolf scratches sting.

"I was trying to save Tumble. I sensed danger in the Pack, danger very close to the pups . . . and in my dream before I caught the snake, I didn't *see* the snake. I saw the bad dog." A cold feeling washed over Storm, as if she was back in the rushing river and the water was closing over her head.

If I'm such a good dog, so protective, why did I let them drive me out? The bad dog is still there . . . close to the pups . . . why did I think that leaving would stop them getting hurt?

"I hate how that Pack treated you," Bella muttered, licking her ear. "You and Arrow are some of the best dogs I know, but their bullying made you doubt your own true natures."

"They were scared," Storm replied. "Dogs were being killed. I can't truly blame them for looking at the biggest, strongest dogs."

"And yet nobody questioned Bruno," Bella growled. "He was one of the largest dogs in the Pack, and he was certainly not a better dog, deep down, than you or Arrow. He shouldn't have been above suspicion just because he wasn't a Fierce Dog!"

But perhaps he wasn't suspected because no dog was making him sound guilty no matter what he did.

Storm took a deep breath. She needed to share what had been troubling her—the strange sense that something was wrong, if only she could put her paw on what it was. . . . Maybe, if she talked to another dog about it, her thoughts might become clearer.

"Bella, I've been wondering . . . if perhaps Breeze is not the dog she appears to be." Bella shot Storm a sharp look, so she rushed on, "I know it sounds strange. She always seemed so nice and she always spoke up for me. But now that I think about it, whenever she spoke on my behalf, somehow the Pack seemed to trust me less. And Arrow told me he once caught her dragging a live rabbit around. . . ."

Storm trailed off. It was sounding flimsy even to her, and she already wished she hadn't said anything.

"It doesn't sound strange." Bella stopped. Storm waited to see what she would say, but Bella didn't go on, just pawed at the crunchy leaves.

"What happened?" Storm prompted.

"I've never even told Arrow this," Bella said. "I didn't want to upset him—or risk him losing his temper and confronting her, when that would just have proved her point. But one time, before any of them knew that Arrow and I were mates, I overheard Breeze talking to Rake. She said Arrow was a dirty Longpaw Fang and a murderer."

"*Breeze?* You're sure it was her?" Storm's heart was beating faster.

Why would she say that?

"Yes," Bella sighed. "And like you say, she was one of the nicer dogs, at least to our faces."

"Did she call Arrow by name?" Storm asked Bella slowly.

Bella thought for a moment, scratching behind her ear with

her back paw. "No," she said eventually. "She just said 'that mongrel Fierce Dog.'"

Storm's stomach dropped as she met Bella's eyes, and Bella's ears pricked in surprise.

"You think she meant you?"

"Has Arrow ever killed another dog?" Storm asked. "Because I *have*. I killed Terror, and Blade. If Breeze thought one of us was a murderer . . . I think it would be me."

"Storm, you're not a murderer," Bella said, sternly. "You killed two bad dogs, both in battle. You made sure that Terror and Blade couldn't hurt any dog anymore. That doesn't make you bad."

"I know," said Storm. But she wondered if every dog saw it that way.

Breeze said one of us was a Longpaw Fang and a murderer. . . .

Breeze hunted for herself, cruelly torturing her prey. . . .

Some dog had been turning the Pack against Storm all this time. Some dog had wanted them all to think that a large, vicious dog had murdered Whisper and Bruno. Some dog who had fooled them all.

She had suspected Terror's Pack, hadn't she? And Breeze was one of them. Woody, Ruff, and Rake had left, which meant they couldn't have killed Bruno or slipped in and out of the Wild

Pack's territory unnoticed as the bad dog had seemed to.

But Breeze had chosen to stay.

So had Chase—but when Storm had confronted Chase, she had been so terrified, so sure that Storm was going to hurt her.

Breeze was never afraid of me, Storm realized. *Not when dogs were killed . . . not even when Daisy told the Pack I was sleepwalking.*

But what did that mean? Did it make her a scheming bad dog, or just a good Packmate? After all, Breeze had always stood up for Storm. Storm remembered the brown dog's face, wide-eyed and creased with concern, looking from Storm to the other dogs, as if she couldn't believe Storm was being accused of anything.

How could that dog, Storm's friend, be bad enough to kill other dogs in cold blood?

It still felt impossible, but Storm forced herself to say it out loud. "*Breeze* could have been the bad dog all along."

Bella chewed at her front paw anxiously. "It's possible. She's the one dog who we know isn't honest."

Breeze *had* always stood up for Storm, but what had she actually said? Wasn't it usually something like, *I don't mean Storm, just a dog as big as Storm* or *Just because Bruno was killed the way Storm killed Terror, it doesn't mean it was her?*

Hadn't Storm already realized some dog had been undermining her the whole time?

A shudder passed through Storm, and she suddenly felt a jittery energy in her paws.

Breeze had always defended Storm, but her comments had always made things worse. Sometimes, Breeze had jumped to defend Storm before any other dog had even mentioned her name. If it hadn't been for Breeze, maybe suspicion wouldn't have fallen on her at all!

"Maybe it was all part of a plan to get me to leave," Storm wondered aloud, "if she really hates me that much. Maybe the bad things have stopped now that I've left."

Bella didn't look convinced.

Or maybe I left the Pack in great danger? An unwelcome thought crept into her mind. *Maybe I shouldn't have left. Perhaps I've doomed them all?* She shook herself, making her cuts sting. *No.*

When I left, it seemed there was no solution, no way of knowing who the traitor was. I would never have learned all this if I hadn't come here.

Certainty settled on her, like snow on the grass. Although excitement was prickling her pelt, inside she felt calmer than she could remember feeling in many moons. "Breeze *is* the bad dog."

"Storm?" said a small voice, and Storm turned to see Nip and Scramble, both sitting right behind her.

"Pups, you shouldn't sneak up on dogs like that," Bella chided gently.

"It's all right," said Storm, leaning down to give the two pups a lick each.

"Storm," said Nip again, putting his tiny nose right up to Storm's much larger one, "did you have a fight?"

"Did you win?" Scramble asked.

"Yes," she said out loud, as she and Bella shared a solemn look. "I fought and won."

I only wish that were true.

Storm lay in the clearing, watching the pups play and letting her wounds heal, until the shadows lengthened and a chill started to creep up from the ground. Arrow returned, his jaws full of prey—not as much as they would have had if Storm had hunted too, but enough to feed them all for the night. He saw Storm's scratches and his eyes went wide, but Bella gave him a sharp look and he didn't ask any questions.

Storm sat and chewed on her mouthful of prey, and watched the rest of her little Pack. Bella was rolling on the ground, with

Scramble bouncing around her as if he was trying to hunt prey ten times his size, his ears flopping around his face as he growled and sprang. Nearer the den, Arrow was showing Nip how he turned a sleep-circle, treading down the ground to make sure it was comfortable, then curling up with his tail under his nose. The tiny puppy tucked his head in so neatly he looked almost like a furry rock, except that his tail was out and thumping happily on the ground.

This Pack needs me too, Storm thought. *But there is no traitor dog here. The pups will be safe with Bella and Arrow, as long as the wolves keep their promises.*

Suddenly, the effort of all this thinking, and of fighting off the wolves and dragging herself back to the camp, caught up with Storm. Her eyes closed, and opening them again was like climbing a steep hill.

"All right, let's get inside. We all need to rest, especially Storm," said Bella, throwing a stern glance at Storm. Storm nodded and turned toward the den she had made for herself behind the wall of vines. But before she ducked inside and turned her sleep-circle, she stopped and looked up at the sky between the tall trees. There were no clouds tonight, and faint twinkling lights winked at her from the deep darkness.

Sky-Dogs, she thought. *You see everything. Please, if the Wild Pack is in danger, if I should go back, send me a sign. . . .*

Storm woke up to the sensation of damp under her and a chill in her bones. She hadn't dreamed at all, that she could remember, but she didn't feel as if she had rested well either. Her legs seemed to creak as she stood up and trod down the ground around her bedding of leaves and moss. It must have rained hard in the night, and the water had soaked through the earth to reach her sheltered den.

She stretched and stepped outside. The leaves didn't crunch anymore; instead they were like soft mulch under her paws, disintegrating into the mud wherever she walked. Wisps of mist had collected in the hollow, and they swirled and backed away from Storm when she breathed near them.

The light from the Sun-Dog hadn't found its way down here yet. Storm looked up, and a prickling unease ran all the way down her back from the tips of her ears to her stiff tail.

The light was red, deeper and darker than she thought light could be.

Storm scrambled to the top of the slope and looked out. The whole sky was bloodred. The Sun-Dog was starting to poke his ears over the horizon, but they were a fiery dark orange, and the clouds were lit up with burning bright lines of red and gold.

Blood and fire. That can only mean danger.

"I understand," Storm whispered. Her heart was racing. "The Pack is in danger. *Terrible* danger. I must go back."

She stood there a moment longer, held down by the weight of the Sky-Dogs' answer.

"You wouldn't show me this if it was too late," she barked at the sky. "I have a long way to go, but there's still hope! There must be!"

As she watched, holding her breath for a response from the Sky-Dogs, she realized that already the bloodred sky was fading back into the clear blue of a new morning.

Storm stretched, testing her muscles. Her paws, at least, didn't hurt anymore. That was good. She would be able to travel, even if her wolf wounds still ached.

She needed to eat, and then she needed to leave.

She returned to the camp as the Sun-Dog was peeking down into the clearing over the tops of the trees, and laid her catch down in the empty cleared space that was the small Pack's prey pile. She had hunted alone, up the slope away from the wolves' territory, and had been relieved to find there were signs of prey there, enough burrows and nests to keep the pups fed for a little while. She had caught a dozy rabbit and several large mice.

"Storm? You've been hunting early. Are you feeling better?" asked Bella, stretching and yawning as she came out of the den.

Storm sat back on her haunches as Arrow came after her and the pups followed them on wobbly, sleepy legs.

"Bella, Arrow. I need to tell you something," she said.

The two dogs looked at each other, their ears pricking up in surprise. "Sounds serious," muttered Arrow. "Is everything all right?"

"Storm, are you . . . leaving us?" Bella whined.

"Not for good," Storm said. "But yes. I have to go. If I don't, I'm afraid Breeze will hurt the pups, or even destroy the Pack. They weren't kind to me, but they need my help, so I have to go."

She looked at the two pups, watching her from behind their parents' tails.

"I won't stay there. This is my Pack now. I'll be back as soon as I can."

"Storm," said Arrow, "are you sure? You could be putting yourself in danger going back there. How are you sure it's Breeze?"

"I'm sure," Storm replied. "Bella can tell you."

"I'd say we would come with you," Bella whined. "You shouldn't have to do this on your own—but the pups are too small to travel so far."

"I know," Storm said, her heart swelling. "Don't worry about me. You look after the pups, and each other, and I'll be back before you know it."

"You're a part of this Pack too, you know," Arrow said. "It isn't us and the pups, plus you. It's all of us, and we stand together." He glanced at Bella and then went on. "I know you'll do what you have to do. But we won't just let you go off thinking you're alone. If you're not back after ten journeys of the Sun-Dog, we will come and find you."

"That's right," Bella said. She walked up to Storm and pressed the top of her head against Storm's neck, comforting and stern all at the same time.

Storm felt as if joy and sadness were filling her up, starting at her paws and washing right up to her ears.

"I . . . I don't know what to say."

Arrow came up beside his mate and rested his chin on Storm's shoulder.

"You don't need to say anything. Just hurry back."

Storm pulled away at last. "I will."

"And don't let my litter-brother or his mate push you around," said Bella, her eyes wide with worry. "If they won't listen to you . . . well, you *make* them listen."

I'll have to, Storm thought. *I don't know if any dog will believe what I have to say. After all, I can barely believe it myself.*

She bent her head so she was on eye level with the two pups, who were whispering to each other. "Pups? I need to go away for a little while. Will you come and say good-bye?"

Nip and Scramble bounced up to her and head-butted her legs, their tails wagging. Storm licked them each in turn.

"Good-bye, Nip. Good-bye, Scramble."

"Don't forget Tufty," Nip barked.

"Storm is in a hurry, Nip," Bella chided him gently.

Storm sighed, but she might as well indulge the pups just this once.

"Good-bye for now, Tufty," she said, looking slightly to one side of Nip and hoping she had gotten the right place. The pups seemed satisfied. "Be good. I'll miss you all."

"It's okay, Storm," said Scramble seriously. "Tufty will visit you. She'll tell us you're okay."

"Er . . . good. Thanks, Tufty," Storm said awkwardly. *I love these pups,* she thought. *I just wish they were a little less . . . creepy.* "I'll see you all soon."

"Good luck," said Bella, stepping back. "Spirit Dogs go with you."

"Go quickly, and may the Watch-Dog guide your pawsteps," Arrow added in a low voice. "If you're really going to face the bad dog, you'll need all the help you can get."

"Thanks," Storm said, and turned away before she could change her mind. She had to do this. When she got to the top of the slope, she looked back just once at the worried, hopeful faces of her Packmates before walking away.

She only hoped she wasn't already too late.

CHAPTER SIXTEEN

Storm tried to focus on saving her energy as she ran through the steep woods, scrambling down slopes and then clambering up over rocks. She couldn't sprint headlong toward the Pack, not with the wolf scratches that might reopen if she wasn't at least a little careful. She would be no use to them if she arrived all dizzy and sick from the wounds going bad.

She focused on her paws hitting the ground, on the feeling of her aching wounds itching as they began to heal, and on making sure she kept scenting around—the last thing she needed was to stray onto wolf territory again. She kept far away from the stream, veering so far from it that she was almost running in the wrong direction to get back to the Wild Pack's camp. She had to find the Endless Lake—that was the quickest way. She could just follow the sandy shoreline and the cliffs all the way back. It had taken her many journeys of the Sun-Dog to get here, but she hadn't been trying to go fast then. If she kept her focus and only paused to rest and eat, she might even make it back to the Light House before the Sun-Dog went down to his den beyond the sea. As long as she didn't get distracted—or killed by angry wolves along the way.

And of course, if she could *find* the Endless Lake.

She paused, though it was frustrating to have to stop moving when the Sun-Dog would not. The Endless Lake scent was here, she could smell it, but it was annoyingly vague. She wasn't on very familiar territory, and while she couldn't scent wolves, she couldn't scent much else either except for pine trees and the old trails of creatures who had already moved on.

"Come on," she muttered, sniffing the air, then turning her nose to the ground, and then to the sides of the trees. "Wind-Dogs, help me—where is the lake?"

There was no extra breath of wind as an answer, but a moment later Storm's ears pricked up as a harsh squawk rang through the air from somewhere to her left. Her head twisted around, pulling uncomfortably at the scab that was forming over her shoulder wound.

"The white birds!" she yapped. "Thank you, Wind-Dogs!" *I'd know that annoying noise anywhere.* Turning toward it with a new

221 🐕

spring in her step, she put on an extra burst of careful speed.

Storm soon found her muzzle filling with the salty scent of the Endless Lake as she followed the sound of the birds, and finally the trees thinned and turned to low scrubby bushes. Just as Storm noticed that the ground under her paws was becoming rocky and sandy, the land in front of her fell away in a rough slope and she saw the Endless Lake.

The Wind-Dogs were busy here, sending a stiff breeze along the shore that ruffled Storm's fur. Choppy waves were lashing the sand, and the white birds wheeled unsteadily against the current. It wasn't as warm beside the water as it had been when she'd been traveling the other way, but it wasn't as cold as the dark days and nights of her first Ice Wind either.

That may still be on its way . . . but as long as the water isn't frozen under my paws, I'll be fine.

At least finding her way back would be simple now. Storm turned to her left, knowing that if she kept the lake on her right she would come to the Light House, and then to the Wild Pack's camp.

And then what?

The wind ruffled her fur and she felt her cuts sting in the salty air. Would she have scars? She felt some of the scratches might be deep enough. And she wasn't sure her tail would ever bend quite the same way again.

It was easier to concentrate on those things—real, definite things—than to think too hard about what she had learned from Bella and Arrow, and the terrible conclusion that had settled in her heart.

How was she going to make the Pack believe her? Storm could remember the oppressive fear that had surrounded the Pack for many moons. How could any dog think straight in such a place?

Storm paused to sniff at a pool of water that had formed between a cluster of rocks. It was fresh, not salty lake water, so she lapped up as much of it as she could.

What she had learned from Bella and Arrow had made everything clear. But would the Wild Pack believe information from another Fierce Dog and his mate? She climbed up a grassy slope and found herself on a windswept cliff top with a sheer drop down to the lake. With the Wind-Dogs buffeting her ears and a clear path along the cliff, it was easy to break into a measured run. Storm glanced out at the lake, vanishing over the horizon, and the huge, empty wetness of it felt slightly calming.

She felt as if her mind and her body were running at the same speed now, the rhythmic pounding of her paws and the rasp of her breath seeming to echo the sound of her thoughts running through her head.

How can I get them to listen to me? It sounds so unlikely. Breeze seems such a gentle dog. Is it all an act? What about the pups? Breeze loves the pups . . . doesn't she?

She spent a lot of time with them. And they seemed to like her. But now that suddenly felt quite sinister to Storm. All dogs thought being good with pups was the sign of a good dog, and yet . . .

Storm hadn't been as close with Lucky and Sweet's pups in their early days as she had with Nip and Scramble. Now she knew just how suggestible pups were, how easily they made friends with anything that would stand still long enough.

Just look at Tufty, she thought. *They heard that they had a sister, and they invented an invisible pup who could play with them.*

And what about the stories Breeze told them?

When Storm wanted Nip and Scramble to go to sleep, she told them quiet stories about birds in their nests and rabbits in their holes. When she wanted them to hurry, she told them about the Wind-Dogs hunting the Golden Deer, and the tiny pups took it all in, and now they told those stories to each other—and to Tufty—so often that Bella had had to stop them rushing off to find the Deer all by themselves, even though they were barely the size of a full-grown deer's head.

And what had Breeze told the pups about?

The secret world in the lake, under the water, where the Sun-Dog went to play every night. Was it any wonder that the pups wanted to go there and find it for themselves? Shouldn't some dog have made sure they didn't think it was real?

Storm looked down at the water of the lake crashing against the cliff.

They could have drowned. Tiny nearly did *drown.*

But Breeze was there to save them. . . .

Storm put on a burst of speed, ignoring the pulling and stinging of her wounds now. She felt urgency running through her bones as the landscape around her blurred and her ears flapped in the wind.

Did she intend them to drown? Or did she always intend to save them? Did she care either way?

The cliff ended in a steep slope down to the beach, and Storm scrambled down it.

I have no proof of any of this. Kind, gentle, helpful Breeze? The Patrol Dog who's never been seen to hurt a rabbit, let alone another dog? No dog would believe it.

I need a plan. The sand curved inward here, and as Storm trotted over it, she realized there was a thin stream of cool water running through it. She looked up toward its source and hesitated. It was trickling from a large opening, as round as a ripe berry, made from the same kind of hardstone as the long-paw paths and dens.

She sighed. Longpaws were always making things so much bigger than they were. Digging this hole must have taken whole journeys of the Moon-Dog, just to make a special underground river for this water to flow down.

As if Breeze wasn't enough, she found herself worrying about the longpaws again. What would happen if they wanted to dig tunnels like this under the Wild Pack, or build dens or drive their loudcages up and down the cliff?

She sniffed carefully around the circular hole. The water didn't smell bad—a little musty from running over hardstone, but not sick. She splashed into the middle of the shallow stream and rolled over carefully. The cool water felt wonderful on her wolf wounds.

But as she was getting up, a splash of water went up her nose and she spluttered, and then another memory struck her:

Breeze had been attacked by the bad dog, hadn't she? She'd

been dragged through the territory in the night, and almost drowned in the river.

The dogs probably thought Storm had done it in her sleep. . . .

Storm gazed down at her reflection in the little stream, splintering like broken clear-stone around her paws.

"No other dog saw her attacker. No dog caught their scent," she muttered. A drip of water ran down her face and she shook herself, spraying water and making her fur stand on end.

There was a trail, like something had been dragged. Breeze was wet and scratched.

"She could have done it herself," Storm whispered. "She could *easily*. A dog who's willing to murder her Packmates, put clear-stone and poison in the prey pile, lie and manipulate and try to drown four innocent pups? Of *course* she could have left that trail herself."

Storm scrabbled out of the stream and trotted along the sand.

Breeze and the Fear-Dog are connected. She did all of this to make us afraid, to make us turn on each other. It's like she's . . . she's feeding the Fear-Dog!

Why else would any dog cover their camp in rabbit blood? No dogs had actually been hurt, and no strange scents were found, but the blood was . . . *wrong*. It frightened the dogs, set them all on edge. It couldn't have been done with prey that was killed out in the fields and dragged back, it had to be . . .

"A live rabbit," Storm howled to the sky in anger and frustra-tion. *"She was carrying a live rabbit!"*

It had happened just after Bella and Arrow had left the Pack. The timing was right. Arrow had seen Breeze running back to camp with a live, suffering rabbit between her jaws. Breeze had claimed to be with the pups when it had happened, and they'd all taken her word for it. But the pups had been asleep in their den, and even if they woke up, they were too small to understand that they should tell another dog if Breeze wasn't there.

Storm followed the sand around a rocky outcrop, and all of a sudden she could see something in the distance, right at the edge of the water, almost too small to make out.

The Light House! For once, Storm thanked the Spirit Dogs that the longpaws did like to put their huge, immovable paw prints all over the landscape—they couldn't have known it, but their mysterious Light House would show her the way back to her Pack.

I still have no proof, she thought. *They'll say I could come up with the same kind of suspicions about any dog in the Pack.*

But now when Storm imagined Breeze's brown eyes gazing at her, she didn't feel friendship or kindness. All she felt was her hackles rising.

CHAPTER SEVENTEEN

Storm climbed up onto a pile of large, wide rocks, startling a white bird she hadn't even been trying to catch. The Sun-Dog was peeking over the trees, about to start his long run across the sky, and his pale light gleamed against the tall white Light House. She was almost there.

She had stopped and slept when the Sun-Dog had vanished under the water of the lake, curling up in a sandy hollow sheltered by thick reeds. It made no sense to push on through the darkness and arrive at the Pack exhausted.

Still, even though she had rested, her paws were aching, and all her muscles felt tense, as if she had been crouching to spring for a long time without release.

I made it this far, she thought. *I didn't run into the wolves, or the long-paws—or Pistol and Dagger.*

She had been turning her theories and ideas over and over in her mind before she slept, and after she got moving again. Now she found herself thinking about the two Fierce Dogs. They really were the kind of dogs some of the Pack had expected her and Arrow to be: vicious, dangerous, untrustworthy, loyal to their crazed Alpha above all.

Once, Storm would have worried the Wild Pack dogs might be right. What if she couldn't control her more violent urges?

She didn't feel like that now.

Storm stepped onto the hardstone path to the Light House once more. Its mysterious light was still blazing, even though the Sun-Dog was awake. It flashed over the Endless Lake and then over the land in an endless circle. Storm remembered that after the Storm of Dogs, she'd thought it was a sign that Martha and their other friends would always be with them, watching over them. It was a comforting idea. Perhaps Martha was with her now, willing her to get back to the Pack in time.

I had to leave before I could find the bad dog. I'm glad I've got a new Pack now, but I still have to help the Wild Pack, if I can. The landscape became more and more familiar as she pressed on, though it had changed a little while she was away. When she had left, it had been Long Light and everything had been green and lush. Now the wind was cooler and the leaves on the trees were blazing red and brown in the first rays of the Sun-Dog.

She began to pick up the faint scents of dogs, although she wasn't yet in their territory—they had hunted here, perhaps a few journeys of the Sun-Dog ago.

She couldn't pick out their individual scents, but the familiarity of the Pack scent sparked feelings that Storm thought she had left behind forever.

She found herself thinking of the four pups, clambering over her and over one another. Sweet's thoughtful face as she tried her best to make the right decisions for the Pack. Daisy and Sunshine yapping and turning overexcited circles. Mickey's kindly face and Snap's bark, so loud and fearless for a small dog.

And Lucky . . .

He raised me. And he did it well, too. He taught me to do what was needed to protect my Pack, and to stand up for myself. Why couldn't he see that I was the last dog who would turn traitor against him and Sweet?

Did he really think she was like Pistol and Dagger, and the other Fierce Dogs of Blade's Pack? And those Fierce Dogs weren't even like the bad dog—they had never betrayed their own Pack. Even after the defeat they suffered on the frozen river, even though Blade was *dead*, they were so loyal to her that they'd tried to kill Storm in revenge!

Some of the dogs in the Wild Pack could learn something about loyalty from them, Storm thought, looking around warily at the familiar rolling fields, as if a nearby dog might overhear her rebellious private thoughts.

Storm's path led her along another cliff, beside a field where she remembered hunting with the Wild Pack. Sure enough, there were the faint traces of dog-scents, overlaid with a much stronger scent of rabbit.

Storm's mouth watered. She hadn't eaten since she set out from Bella and Arrow's camp, and she needed to keep her strength up—for the rest of the walk to the Wild Pack, and for whatever happened afterward.

She lowered her belly close to the ground and crept into the thinning grass of the field, sniffing for the rabbit, her ears pricked up for any sound and to make sure she kept upwind. The Wind-Dogs were rushing about, blowing across the surface of the lake and playing around on the cliffs, so it was hard to be sure that the rabbit wouldn't smell her—she just had to hope that the confusion of scents swirling around it would conceal her if she kept moving.

After a few more pawsteps, she saw it huddling under a bush, sheltering from the wind.

I'll have to get as close as I can, Storm thought. *No wolf is going to run this rabbit down if I lose it.*

But if she circled around the bush, approaching the rabbit from the other side . . .

Stepping carefully to avoid the leaves that would crunch loudly under her paws and give her away if she trod on them, Storm rounded the bush, paused, took a deep breath, and sprang.

The rabbit tried to run, but it was caught in its own hiding place. By the time it had almost wriggled its way out of the bush, Storm's paws and then her teeth had come down on it. She dragged it out and shook it hard to kill it as cleanly as she could.

She tucked in immediately, filling her belly and relishing the warmth and satisfaction of a good hunt. When she was done, she looked down at the remains of the prey and shook herself, trying not to think of the sad, wriggling thing that Breeze must have carried all the way back to the Pack camp.

Even if all her worst suspicions were true, and Breeze was behind everything that had gone wrong in the Pack since the Storm of Dogs . . . the killings, the sabotage, and other things too, like trying to push those rocks down on Moon and even framing her for stealing prey . . .

Storm still hadn't figured out *why*. What could make a dog like

Breeze decide that instead of being a good Packmate, she would devote herself to spreading fear, chaos, and death?

It had to be something to do with the Fear-Dog. Breeze was one of the dogs who had come from Terror's Pack. They had all been filled with a dread of the Spirit Dog Terror had invented. Storm remembered that Breeze had been so scared, she didn't even want him to be named before the Great Howl. She believed in him, that was for sure.

Could all of this be about Terror after all?

Storm started to walk again, following the familiar lines of the landscape, but not running at full speed anymore.

If a dog could be loyal to a leader as cruel as Blade, after all, she supposed one could be loyal to the crazed Terror, who had believed he was possessed by the spirit of the Fear-Dog. Storm shuddered at the memory of facing the huge dog: he'd suffered from fits that left him foaming at the mouth, and he'd ruled his Pack through sheer dread, turning on his own dogs with unpredictable fits of rage, scaring them into attacking the Wild Pack because they knew that it was safer to run into battle than disobey him.

But even though they had finally turned on him and joined the Wild Pack, Terror's dogs had found some kind of home with him. He took in broken dogs, lone dogs, dogs who had already been rejected by other Packs or lost their homes. That would inspire loyalty of a sort, even if it was twisted and terrible.

"Broken dogs . . . ," Storm muttered. She had been thinking of Twitch, who had left the Wild Pack with a terrible limp and came back on three legs. But what if a dog was broken on the *inside*? What if there was a dog who had truly respected Terror and believed in his ways?

She would take his death . . . badly.

For a dog she'd counted as a friend, Storm realized it was strange that Breeze had never told her anything about her life before Terror. The other dogs had never talked about what her role was in his Pack. Terror didn't have a real Beta, as far as she knew. . . .

But there are a lot of things I didn't know that I do know now.

Storm hopped up onto the log of a fallen tree and looked out across the fields. There was a line of trees, and beyond the woods she knew there was the hill, the pond, and the Wild Pack camp.

"I'm back," she barked aloud, testing out how it sounded. "I think you're in danger. I think it's Breeze. . . ."

She didn't need to say any more. She knew that she wouldn't get a chance to list all the reasons she suspected the brown dog—if she wasn't certain, and she didn't have any proof, the dogs would never accept her theory. All she would get was an argument, and they might even chase her away.

I need to know more, and there are only a few dogs who can answer my questions.

She turned away from the Endless Lake and put her nose to the ground, sniffing at the faint dog-scent. If she searched the hunting fields and the woods, she should be able to find her way.

She needed to talk to Breeze's old Pack. *Terror's* Pack.

I just hope I haven't misjudged them the way I misjudged Breeze.

CHAPTER EIGHTEEN

Storm had traveled so far in the past two journeys of the Sun-Dog, her paw pads were aching. They stung even more now that she was moving more slowly. She crisscrossed the land, stopping all the time to sniff and search for any sign of Rake, Ruff, Woody, or Dart. When she'd been pounding along the cliffs beside the Endless Lake, she had felt as light as a floating leaf, and it had been obvious that she was making progress, despite the pain from her wolf wounds. Now her paws hurt, too, and every time she thought she had found the trail, it escaped her again.

Circling the Wild Pack's territory, even keeping a wide stretch of land between her and the camp, brought back powerful memories. There was the valley where, after a long chase, the Golden Deer had led them to a herd of ordinary deer, and there was the field where she'd brought the first hunting party she ever led by herself.

There were painful memories here too. At one point the land sloped away and she could see the overhang by the river where the Wild Pack had made their stand against the Fierce Dogs, leading them into an ambush. She remembered the whispers and worries about accepting the three Fierce pups into the Pack, let alone battling Blade to protect them. And here and there she found strange half memories of places she had been in her sleep. . . .

Finally, as the Sun-Dog was getting low in the sky, she sniffed around the trunk of a large tree, and she caught a scent she would know anywhere.

Dart.

Storm had drawn near the forest where she had seen Chase meet up with her old Packmates. She had to be close now. The thin dog's scent was strong, and fresh, and Storm was starting to follow it when a dog's bark rang out behind her.

"Stop there, Fierce Dog!"

Storm turned slowly. The last thing she wanted to do was look threatening right now. Dart was standing behind her, with Ruff by her side. The two dogs both seemed smaller than Storm remembered. Dart had always been thin, but Storm thought she looked hungrier now than the last time she'd seen her, and Ruff was just a small black ball of fur with pale amber eyes, easily mistaken for a pup if a dog didn't know better.

"Hello, Dart," Storm said, making sure to keep her voice low, without a hint of a growl.

"Stay where you are," Ruff barked. "Don't move. Rake and Woody are within barking distance, and you can't fight all four of us at once."

Are you sure? Storm thought, remembering her battle against the wolves. But she couldn't say anything like that, no matter how tempting it was. Instead she lowered her head, and then lay down with her belly on the grass.

"I'm not here to fight you," she said.

"Chase said you left the Wild Pack," Dart whined. "We thought you'd gone far away. What are you doing here?"

Storm hesitated for a second, wondering what these dogs would believe. Rake and Woody she had thought of as friends, once. The same couldn't be said for Dart—she had never liked Storm, or either of her brothers.

Storm decided that honesty, as strange as it sounded, was all she had left.

"I've come back to fight the bad dog," she said.

She could tell from the look that Dart gave her, eyes bulging out of her thin face, that the she thought Storm was lying. *I guess you thought I was the bad dog,* she thought.

"I think I know who it is," Storm went on. "I went away and found some things out, and I couldn't leave the Pack in danger. But I need your Pack's help."

As she waited for the dogs to respond, Storm's throat seemed to close up. She had to remind herself to keep breathing. She wished it was Rake who'd found her—it suddenly seemed as if the lives of the Pack might depend on what Dart, of all dogs, chose to do now.

"We haven't heard of any problems in the Pack since you left," Dart sneered. "They're just fine without you—and look at you, with all those wounds and scars. I think it's best if you go back to whatever Fierce Dog place you've been hiding. We don't need a savage dog in our territory."

Storm let out a heavy sigh, suppressing a growl. That was just like Dart. The thin dog thought she was so clever. But if Storm lost her temper, Dart would take it as proof that Fierce Dogs were bad, and she would never get anywhere.

"Please, Dart, just *listen* to me," she said as smoothly as she could. "I know you don't believe me, but the Pack is in trouble—"

"I'm sure they are!" Dart snarled. "If you don't leave us all alone!" She barked and snapped at the air—a nice safe distance from Storm's muzzle, Storm noticed, but she still shrank back a little, scenting the anger and fear starting to rise from Dart. The sight of these two small dogs trying to drive her off could have been comical, after she'd faced wolves and Fierce Dogs and even the two longpaws with their silver sticks . . . but all she felt was frustration. That after everything she had been through to try to help, she was still just surrounded by this endless suspicion. She knew she couldn't growl back or they would never listen to her. And that felt so unfair.

Storm got to her paws—slowly, so that Dart wouldn't take it as a challenge—and bowed her head. "I still need your help."

"What help could you possibly need from us?" asked Ruff. Storm's heart leaped. Perhaps Ruff would be curious enough to talk with Storm after all.

But Dart barked again and stepped in front of the little black dog. "We don't care what it is! Get away!" she yapped. Her fear-scent was strong now, her eyes were wide and dark, and her legs were trembling hard. Storm could see that Dart was scared, that staring Storm down one-on-one went against all her instincts, and Storm could almost respect that. No matter how misplaced Dart's fear was . . .

"I'll go for now," she said. "But I need to ask you something, Ruff—and Rake and Woody. Will you tell them?"

Ruff didn't answer; she just growled quietly from behind Dart's shaking legs. Storm backed away, and finally turned her back on the two dogs and walked away into the nearest stand of trees. She walked slowly until she was out of sight and scent of Dart and Ruff, and then curled up in a comfy patch of moss, turning a sleep-circle before she settled down. But she wasn't planning on staying there long.

What do I do? she thought. She felt strangely calm. Dart's attitude was a problem, but wasn't it better to try out her story on the one dog who was least likely to believe her? All she needed to do was find the rest of the Pack and get them to *listen.*

Ruff was halfway there. She wanted to know what I was here to ask. But how can I get their attention without scaring them?

Her stomach rumbled, and Storm's ears pricked up.

"That's it!" she muttered. *They didn't exactly look well-fed. Maybe they've been having trouble hunting. . . .*

Four dogs wasn't many for a Pack, especially when two of them were as fragile as Dart and Ruff. If Storm wanted their cooperation, perhaps she needed to appeal to their appetites.

As the Sun-Dog dipped toward the horizon, Storm padded out of the woods with a couple of squirrels and a weasel dangling from her jaws. They smelled delicious, but she resisted the urge to take a bite.

She followed Dart's and Ruff's scents to their camp easily, even with the tasty prey scents in her mouth. The camp was a little space under the shade of a huge spreading bush, barely a rabbit-chase away from the place they'd caught her. The bush had flowered during Long Light, and now the space underneath it was covered in soft, sweet-smelling petals.

Three of the four dogs were up on their paws by the time she reached them, their ears pricked, and in Dart's case, her teeth bared. Storm padded toward them slowly, but without showing fear, wagging her tail as if she was greeting old friends. Was that a glint of happiness she saw in Rake's eyes as he saw her?

Woody was the only one not standing, and as Storm approached and set her catch down at the edge of the petals, she noticed that he shifted uncomfortably, as if to hide one of his back legs from view.

Perhaps that's why they look so hungry. If Woody's hurt, they only have one competent hunter to feed four dogs.

"Storm," Dart snarled, "I told you to leave us alone!" But Storm saw her gaze flick to the squirrels, and her tongue shot out and licked around her muzzle.

"I brought these for you," Storm said, ignoring Dart and speaking directly to Rake, Woody, and Ruff. "I just want to talk. I promise." She stepped away from the prey and backed off, sitting down out of reach and bowing her shoulders low to the ground.

The dogs stared at one another, and then at the prey. Ruff started toward it, then backed off again.

"Please, take it. I can get more."

Rake huffed at her, blowing the long gray fur on his muzzle, and stepped forward to pick up the prey. "Thank you, Storm," he said, dropping one of the squirrels in front of Woody. Storm watched, interested, as he gave the weasel to Dart and Ruff to share, and took the other squirrel for himself.

Dart held back, her head up haughtily, but Ruff could hardly contain herself. She sniffed at the squirrel, backed off, and then approached it again, before looking up at Rake with watery eyes.

"Are you the Alpha, Rake?" Storm asked.

Rake nodded. "And Woody is my Beta. Ruff is our Omega."

Storm tried not to visibly relax, though relief was flooding through her body. "Then you can decide whether I'm a threat, can't you? All I want is to ask a few questions. You know me, Rake. We shared a Pack once, hunted together, ate together, slept close together in the hunters' den. You were with me when we buried Whisper. You know I didn't kill him."

Rake tilted his head, one ear raised. "I don't know that for certain."

"I'd never hurt any of you," Storm said. *Not even Dart.*

"Alpha, she's a *Fierce Dog*," Dart growled. "Who knows what she would do." But her voice sounded weak, and she looked down at the squirrel in front of her paws again and trailed off.

Storm said nothing. She'd said and done everything she could.

Rake glanced at Woody. Rake's long-furred face didn't give much away, but they seemed to have come to an agreement.

"Ask your questions, then," said Rake. "And we'll take your offering of prey, with thanks. Go ahead," he said to Ruff, whose little black body was practically vibrating with excitement. Ruff set upon the prey with almost savage enthusiasm, and Dart had to snarl at her and shoulder her way in to make sure she got her share.

"Thank you," Storm said, getting up from her position of submission.

Rake and Woody began to eat too, and Storm let them get a few mouthfuls down before she took a deep breath and spoke.

"I want to ask about Breeze. What was it like, being in a Pack with her?"

Rake and Woody both looked up at her with surprised

expressions. Ruff was too busy devouring her squirrel to even do that.

"What do you mean?" Woody barked. "You know what it's like. She chose your Pack, not ours. She's a loyal Packmate. Hard worker."

What did I expect? Storm told herself. *Did I think they would say, oh yes, Breeze is evil, we knew that all along?*

"She's certainly been loyal to Sweet," she said slowly. "Was she . . . just as loyal when you were in a Pack together? With Terror?"

Ruff jumped at the mention of Terror's name and looked up, almost as if she thought he might be here with Storm. Rake cast her a worried look.

"I know you were all loyal Packmates then," she added. "And Chase told me that Terror took her in and protected her, when she had no other dog to look after her. So I understand that. . . ."

"Yes, Breeze was loyal to Terror." Rake shook himself. "Storm . . . we don't talk about that time much. Is this important?"

"Very important," Storm said. "Please, tell me."

Rake shook himself again, as if there was something stuck in his fur that he was trying to dislodge.

"All right, then. You remember that sometimes, he would

order us to do things that were . . . nonsensical. Or dangerous."

"Both," Woody growled. "Often."

"He'd make us attack other dogs, ones who were much bigger, or in larger Packs—like yours. Or he'd say we had to prove how tough we were by going without food."

Ruff whined into her prey, and Storm was suddenly incredibly glad that she had fed these dogs.

"We only obeyed him because we were afraid," Rake said. "At any moment he could be possessed by . . . by his Spirit Dog. And when that happened, some dog would always get hurt. But Breeze was the only one of us who didn't hesitate to follow his orders."

"I remember once, Terror drove her to the edge of a rushing river and ordered her to leap in. He said . . . what was it? 'Pull the tail of the Fear-Dog! Make him hear you!'" Woody licked his muzzle and looked up at Storm. "She was afraid, but . . . excited, at the same time. I've never seen a dog look quite like that. She jumped right away. She almost drowned."

"I never understood it," yapped Ruff. She spoke slowly, as if every word took a huge effort to get out. "We talked about running away. Me and Rake . . . and Whisper. But not Breeze. Even when *he* wasn't there, she was on his side."

"And also, there was . . . ," Rake began. Storm saw Ruff flinch again, as if she knew what he was about to say, and Dart took a few steps to stand close by the little dog's side.

"The punishments," Woody said. "When we disobeyed him, he would always have one of us punish the others."

"And it was Breeze?" Storm prompted. "She was the one he had carry out these . . . punishments?"

"She was such a kind dog," Rake put in. Storm tilted her head at him, unsure how he could say that when he knew what she'd really been like. "It was only when she was doing Terror's bidding that she could be frightening. Without Terror's orders, she was as good a Packmate as you could wish for."

"Is that what you wanted to hear? All Terror's dogs were broken, but you already knew that," Dart sniffed, in a way that would have struck Storm as dismissive and cruel if she hadn't still been standing protectively in front of Ruff. "Breeze is a good dog. If you think she has anything to do with the bad dog, you're barking up the wrong tree. She loves those pups, for one thing. She only stayed with the Wild Pack for them."

Storm's ears pricked up. "Really?"

"Yes. Once she's finished with the pups, she's going to come and join us. She said so," Dart huffed.

"You see, Storm?" Rake said. "She loves pups. Even though

she'd rather come with us, she couldn't leave them. That doesn't sound like a bad dog to me."

Woody and Ruff both nodded, seeming reassured by this, as if they could put the disturbing memories of Terror's Pack behind them.

But Dart's words seemed to echo in Storm's head, as if they'd been barked into the air by the great Alpha Wolf:

Once she's finished with the pups.

"Is that really all you have?" Dart asked. "*Breeze* is the bad dog? Who are you going to accuse next—Sunshine?"

"Breeze was loyal to Terror, beyond what any other dog felt, right?" Storm said, trying to ignore Dart's sneer. "What if she's still angry about his death? What if all of this is about revenge? Twitch, Lucky, Moon, Bella—they were all there when he died, and the bad dog has targeted them all."

"*You* killed Terror," Woody pointed out. He shifted his weight, and Storm saw that his paw was red and raw. "And you haven't been harmed."

"But I have," Storm said quietly. "I was blamed for everything that's gone wrong, until I had to leave the Pack. If Bella and Arrow hadn't already been driven out, I would have had nowhere to go."

Rake looked a little uncomfortable at this, but he said,

"Storm . . . Whisper and Bruno were the ones who were killed, and neither of them had anything to do with Terror's death. Whisper was fighting on his side at the time. Why would Breeze—or any crazy dog—blame him?"

"I—I don't know," Storm admitted. "But they probably got in her way, or something. . . ."

It was a weak explanation, and Storm knew it. She glared at her paws.

I'm sure I'm right! I just don't have all the information yet.

"I need to ask one more thing," she said. "Will one of you come with me to the Wild Pack and tell them what you've just told me? I don't want you to lie or exaggerate. Just tell Sweet about what Breeze was like in Terror's Pack."

The dogs looked at one another, and there was a long silence. Storm's heart sank.

"Thank you for the prey, Storm," Rake said, and it sank even further. "But we don't want to get involved in this. Woody can't walk that far anyway, and Omega and I are both needed here."

Storm didn't protest. She didn't think it would do any good.

"If you want my advice," Woody said gruffly, "I say don't go back at all. Just leave the territory, go back to Bella and Arrow if you can find them. You've been living in exile—the Wild Pack won't listen to you now."

Storm tried not to let her frustration show. She bowed to the four dogs again.

"Thank you for your help," she said. "I'll go now. Spirit Dogs be with you."

"And with you, Storm," said Rake.

Storm turned away and kept her ears pricked and her tail high until the trees had swallowed her and she could no longer hear or smell the camp of petals. Then she allowed herself to growl, low and angry. Her ears flattened and she looked up at the darkening sky.

CHAPTER NINETEEN

Once she's finished with the pups . . .

The words hadn't stopped ringing in Storm's mind all night. She had eaten and then forced herself to curl up and sleep, knowing that running into the Wild Pack camp in the middle of the night would hardly win her any friends. She needed to be careful about this.

But not too careful. Or Breeze might finish the pups before I can finish her.

Storm didn't know, and couldn't guess, exactly what Breeze's plans for the pups were. But she was convinced now that at the very least Breeze didn't *care* whether one or more of them drowned in the Endless Lake, and if she was using them to hurt Lucky, eventually she would decide to do her worst.

When the world was light enough to see again, Storm got up and started to approach the center of the tangle of smells that made up the Wild Pack territory. She wove between the long, thin shadows of trees and crossed a line of scent from a recent patrol, feeling like a trespasser and like she was coming home, all at the same time.

She pushed through some undergrowth, and her paws touched down on a patch of wonderfully soft moss. Storm sniffed, and then froze. She was standing in a tiny clearing beside a large tree, and beside her were two uneven mounds. One was already overgrown, covered in moss and the small green leaves of new plants. The other was barer, still obviously dug up fairly recently.

Whisper and Bruno.

Storm sat down, the breath huffing out of her chest as if she'd been struck in the back by a huge paw.

"Whisper, am I right about this?" she whispered. "Did Breeze kill you both? What can I do to stop her hurting any more dogs?"

There was no reply, and Storm sat there for a little while longer, thinking of her friends—Bruno, the big dog who'd looked at her just like Dart until he'd finally come to his senses and apologized to Storm, and Whisper, the small gray dog who had been so happy to escape Terror's claws that he idolized Storm.

"I'm sorry it took me so long," she said. "But I'm back now, and I'm not leaving again until I've made this right."

Storm barely had to pay attention to where she was going now, her paws seeming to find their own path through the tangled bushes and through the piles of fallen leaves.

She had to get close enough to the Pack that she could see what was going on without them knowing she was there. The edge of these trees would be perfect, as long as no dog came right past her to go hunting.

The plan that had formed in the night was unsteady, but it was the only one Storm could think of that might work.

Don't even go to the Pack. Don't try to tell Lucky or Sweet. Just catch Breeze alone and convince her to leave the Wild Pack forever—whatever it takes.

She couldn't quite imagine what confronting Breeze would be like. It still seemed to Storm that there were two Breezes—the traitor, and the loyal Packmate. Would she still pretend that she was Storm's friend? Or would she turn and attack her?

What if she won't go? Storm wondered. *What am I willing to do? What if she tries to hurt the pups?*

I'm no savage, no matter what some dogs believe. I won't kill Breeze.

Not unless I have to . . .

Storm stayed between the trees, occasionally moving farther back if the wind changed so her scent might be blown toward the Pack camp. From the edge of the wood, she could peer through the undergrowth and see the grassy slope that led up to the camp. Her heart ached as she settled down to watch and saw the dogs moving around, walking down to the pond to drink, setting off on hunts or patrols. She didn't see Breeze all day.

She rolled in the mud and leaves that covered the forest floor and then lay very still, and that seemed to be enough to hide her scent from the Wild Pack. At least, no dog found her, and no alarmed barking came from the camp.

It seemed as if Dart was telling the truth—nothing terrible had happened since she was gone. The camp seemed peaceful. A strange twisting feeling started up in Storm's stomach, as if she was being pulled in two directions at once: it made her uneasy to know that her absence might have prompted the bad dog to stop, but at the same time she was relieved to see all her Packmates safe and well. Her tail wagged despite herself as she saw them gather for their meal: Lucky and Sweet in the middle of the circle, flanked by their pups.

The pups were so big now! Storm could hardly believe they were the same dogs. All of them were taller than Daisy now, even Tiny. It wouldn't be very long now until they'd choose their adult names. Storm's heart ached with the knowledge that—if everything went according to plan—she might save their lives, but she might never speak to them again.

She couldn't hear what the dogs were saying, but Alpha was obviously calling them up in order to eat their fill—the pups were first, tucking in with their tails wagging hard, then Sweet and Lucky, then Twitch, Mickey, Snap . . . each dog stepped up one by one, and each face made Storm sigh. She had known many of these dogs almost all her life. They had been with her through the hardest times, through the half wolf and the Storm of Dogs. She had missed them.

And when I go back to Bella and Arrow, I'll still miss them.

Hardly any of these dogs had tried to be cruel to her—certainly not since Dart left. She didn't think any one of them wanted to believe that she was the traitor. It was just that they wouldn't *listen* to her. They had let their fear lead them, like the Leashed Dogs on their leather straps.

Breeze was right in the middle of the ranks, and when she stepped up to eat, Storm's heart hurt even more. Breeze's short brown fur was neat and clean, her soft face friendly and open. There was no spark of madness or malevolent gaze. She looked . . . happy.

After they ate, Storm watched Lucky playing with the pups,

rolling around in the grass, tumbling down the slope and grabbing one another's scruffs in playful, gentle teeth.

I used to play like that, Storm thought. *But Grunt was always too rough, and Wiggle was too scared. Maybe soon I can play with Nip and Scramble . . . if I make it back to them.*

A ball of white fur bounced along the ground—Sunshine, working hard as usual, bringing new soft bedding to the hunters' and Patrol Dogs' dens. She met Breeze walking the other way and stopped. A chill of fear ran down Storm's spine for a moment.

Don't you dare touch Sunshine! she thought, but at once she knew that Breeze would do nothing of the sort, not yet, not right in the middle of the camp. She couldn't hear them barking, but they looked like they were having a pleasant conversation.

How can she look so peaceful, but be so bad?

Lucky scrabbled up the slope and joined them, his tail wagging. Sunshine bustled off and vanished, and then Mickey barked something and Lucky turned to see what he wanted—turning his back on Breeze.

No! Storm wanted to howl. Her fur prickled painfully along her back. Breeze could leap now. . . .

She won't. That isn't her plan.

I don't think.

257

Still, Storm watched with her heart pounding in her throat until Breeze left, ducking in through the bushy entrance to the Patrol Dogs' den.

He has no idea how much danger he's in, Storm thought, and it made her chest feel tight. *But perhaps he never needs to know. If I can deal with Breeze alone, they can all go on believing . . . believing that I'm the bad dog.*

It was a desperately sad thought, but it didn't make Storm as angry as it would have done before. She was done with trying to explain herself. It didn't matter what they thought of her as long as they were safe.

After all, I have a new Pack now.

The Pack were all settling down now, making their way to their respective dens. The pups' game was slowing down: Storm saw Tiny leap on Fluff's unsuspecting back, but then slide off again with a huge yawn. Storm found herself yawning too. Her eyelids felt heavy. She had traveled so far in so few days, and Breeze was quiet in her den, surrounded by dogs.

It wouldn't hurt just to close her eyes for a moment. . . .

The Moon-Dog was hiding her nose, only a thin arc of bright silver showing in the sky. The light she cast was strong, but somehow sickly and cold. Storm tried to focus on the camp. There were distant shifting shapes at its edge, but when Storm looked directly at them, they seemed to flit away.

She was concentrating so hard, she wasn't sure when the noise began—it was a soft crunching at first, like red leaves under the paws of a heavy dog, then a louder, closer breaking of twigs. Something large was pushing through the undergrowth, coming nearer and nearer. Storm couldn't turn her head to look at it; she could only crouch with her gaze fixed on the darting shadows at the camp while it lumbered closer.

It was nearly on her now. She could hear its wet, rasping breath.

Now she could turn, but she was too late. The shape had passed her, plodding through the trees. It was circling the Wild Pack. For a moment, it was lost in the shadows, but then it stepped into a patch of moonlight and its coat glowed pale yellow.

It was Terror.

Horror crawled in Storm's belly like flies over a piece of long-dead prey. She watched, frozen, as he poked his drooling snout out of the undergrowth and snarled at the camp. Then he turned and continued on his way. He was circling the Wild Pack, stalking them, closer and closer. Storm tried to bark, to raise the alarm, but when she opened her jaws, no sound came out.

Terror's pale fur flashed again in the moonlight, and then a shadow fell across Storm's vision. Her belly was pressed to the ground, her ears flat to her head, and she trembled as the Fear-Dog stalked by. He seemed to be made of pure nothingness, darker than the shadows of the forest could ever be, and Storm knew in her bones that even though she could see the edges of him, in some much truer *way he was far larger and stranger than she could ever understand.*

He didn't look at her, but Storm still began to shake, on the edge of panic, still frozen to the spot and unable to howl a warning to her Pack. She knew he wouldn't attack a dog, if he wanted to kill them—his sheer presence was enough to drive them mad. . . .

She awoke with a start and a whimper, scrabbling to her paws and blinking in the light of the Sun-Dog. Her heart was rattling in her chest and she felt dizzy as she spun around on the spot, still half expecting to see the Fear-Dog creeping between the trees.

It was just a dream. I haven't even walked anywhere, I just slept through the night. . . .

But some dog was barking. Storm's ears pricked up and she stood at alert, her bent tail stiff and lashing at her legs. She was almost overcome with the urge to howl a warning now that she had control of her own voice, but then she realized what the dogs were barking.

"We'll be back soon!" That was Lucky.

Four dogs were bounding down the slope, their ears flopping and their tongues hanging out with happiness. Storm threw herself back down into a crouch and peered through the twigs of a bush.

Her heart ached. The bad dog hadn't attacked in the night.

Her old Packmates seemed safe and well. They seemed happy.

They don't miss me, she thought. It hurt, to face the fact that life had simply gone on without her.

Did they all think she really was the bad dog now?

The four dogs yapped to one another as they headed out in search of prey, and Storm caught her breath as she saw who was in the hunting party: Lucky, Mickey, Snap, and Breeze.

Storm bared her teeth, a thin growl escaping her throat.

They may not realize it, but they still need me.

Breeze must be their scout dog. That meant soon she would split off from the party, running fast and far to scent out the best hunting places. She would be alone.

As soon as the dogs were out of sight, Storm got up and stretched hugely, joints in her back and legs clicking out satisfyingly. She shook herself hard to throw off the last of the darkness from her dream and began to follow the dogs.

She was going hunting too.

CHAPTER TWENTY

Storm had never really hunted another dog before, and it was harder than she had imagined. Prey creatures were alert and wary of their surroundings, but they were usually focused on eating whatever was in front of their noses, or gathering sticks and grass for their nests. The dogs ran with their heads raised, tasting the air all the time for scents being blown from far away, stopping and looking around, alert for any movement.

Storm had to stay on guard all the time, sneaking into cover whenever she could and keeping herself downwind of the hunting party. At one point, as the four dogs were crossing a wide field full of late-blooming yellow flowers, the Wind-Dogs abruptly turned and ran in the opposite direction. Storm's paws kicked up dirt as she bolted for shelter. She hunkered there, her heart in her mouth, as Lucky raised his muzzle to the sky and paused as if he had smelled something strange. Then he shook himself and caught up with the others.

Storm followed carefully, skirting around the field just to be sure. She couldn't let them catch her—she had no excuse for trespassing here, or for tracking them, that any of them would believe.

It seemed to take forever, but finally the four dogs paused under the shade of a tree with blazing red leaves. Storm couldn't hear what they said, but she saw Breeze nod, and Mickey's ears twitch with amusement, and then Breeze was off and running in one direction while the other three headed in another. Breeze moved fast, like a scout dog should, to cover more ground in her search for prey. Storm scrambled to run after her, suddenly afraid that now her chance had come, she would manage to lose her.

Breeze shot across another field and vanished into a thicket of trees, and Storm barreled after her. It wasn't easy to keep up. Breeze seemed to be heading somewhere in particular, by the way she squeezed through bushes and leaped over rocks, hardly stopping to scent the air or look around her. Storm bounded and scrambled along behind. Caution lost out to the worry that Breeze might vanish and Storm would be right back where she started.

She followed Breeze into the woods and was forced to slow down as she found herself facing a tangle of branches. Every way she turned, she ran into another twisted tree or thorny bush, and by the time she fought her way through to a more open space, she had lost sight of the scout dog.

Spirit Dogs, no, Storm thought, her teeth gritted, desperately scenting the air. Then there was a rustle and a startled cheeping sound as a flurry of small birds took off from the trees, just to her right. Storm sprang toward them, pounding through a flurry of fallen leaves. If she hurried, she might catch Breeze's scent.

A clearing opened up in front of Storm, and she almost fell over her own paws as she realized that Breeze was there, sitting in the thin grass with her back to Storm.

What's she doing?

Storm stepped quietly between the trees and into the sunny open space.

"Hello, Storm," said Breeze, without turning around.

Storm froze. A prickling feeling crawled underneath her fur, like an army of ants marching across her back. She was suddenly, painfully aware that she'd been so focused on the chase that she hadn't worked out what she would say to Breeze when she did catch her.

Well, this is it. There's no point in hiding now.

"Hello, Breeze," she said, walking farther out of the shadows.

Breeze turned around. Storm was startled to see that her expression was full of joy, her tongue lolling happily from her jaws as she padded across the clearing, her eyes shining. "It's so good to see you again, Storm!" she yapped, and before Storm could react or pull away, Breeze had given her a kindly lick on the nose. "Are you all right? Why are you here?"

Storm stared at Breeze, feeling almost as frozen to the spot as she had been in her dream. For a moment she actually found herself trying to come up with a polite, friendly greeting.

Then she thought about Whisper's grave, already pushing up thick new growth. She thought about Tiny, half-drowned because she followed a story into the lake. Bruno's jaw ripped clean off, Twitch's agony as the sharp clear-stone pieces stuck into his mouth . . . the happy, peaceful Pack that they could have been, with a place for Storm, and for Arrow and Bella.

If they hadn't been driven out, would Bella's birth still have gone wrong? Would Tufty be alive right now?

Even with Breeze's pleasant, hopeful face in front of her, looking as soft and friendly as ever, Storm growled.

"I know, Breeze," she said. "I know you killed Whisper and Bruno."

She watched the smaller dog carefully. Breeze tilted her brown head, her eyes wide and her ears pricked up in surprise.

Then she barked out a laugh.

"How funny," she said. "That it should be you who figured it out! I never thought of you as particularly bright." She wagged her tail like an eager pup. "Whisper and Bruno both had to die. They were the first—but they won't be the last, of course. That will be you, Storm, I hope."

Storm felt strangely light, as if this couldn't really be happening. The horror of Breeze's friendly, calm expression as she talked about murdering two innocent dogs made Storm's paws itch with the urge to back away.

"You're the bad dog," Storm growled, forcing herself to stay exactly where she was. "It's because of Terror, isn't it? You were loyal to him, and this is all your revenge. You're planning to kill the dogs who were involved in his death."

"Oh, but it's so much more than that. Let me help you," Breeze said, but now there was an edge in her voice, and her open expression turned to a slight snarl. "Terror knew the truth. We both did. There's nothing glorious or terrible about a simple death. But a long life, plagued by *fear* . . . or a death that inspires fear in other dogs . . . those are precious to him."

"The Fear-Dog," Storm prompted. Part of her was howling to

move, to attack, to *do something*, but she ignored the dread pooling in her stomach and kept still, waiting for Breeze's reply.

"You murdered my Alpha, the only other dog who ever understood the Fear-Dog," Breeze went on. She sat down in the grass, as if they were having a nice chat about the best way to hunt squirrels, instead of talking about the murders of their Packmates. "I couldn't simply *kill* you. That wouldn't please the Fear-Dog at all. I promised him that I would tear your Pack apart, make them afraid of their prey, their territory, even each other. For your crime, every dog you care about, and every dog who stood by while my Alpha was murdered, will know terrible suffering," she added. "I've been biding my time, working on my next move. I'm looking forward to watching Lucky realize his precious pups are gone forever. The Fear-Dog will be pleased."

You will never touch those pups again, Storm thought. But to threaten Breeze now would cut off her mad, rambling explanation, and there were answers Storm still needed.

"But Whisper didn't kill Terror—he was in *your* Pack before he was in ours," Storm whimpered.

For an instant it was almost as if Breeze had vanished and been replaced by a different dog—her fangs bared, her eyes opened wider than Storm had ever seen, and she twitched and snapped at the air in front of her. "Do not talk of that pathetic dog," she howled. Then she seemed to get control of herself again, and the snarling maw melted back into a mild, open expression.

What was that? Storm thought, trying not to look as horrified as she felt. Suddenly she understood, deep in her belly, how a smaller dog like Breeze could have taken down a much bigger dog like Bruno. *Was that face the last thing Whisper and Bruno ever saw?*

They must have been so afraid.

"Why, then?" she prodded Breeze. "If he was so pathetic, why bother killing him?"

The alarming snarl didn't come back over Breeze's face, but her ears twitched in agitation.

"Because he wouldn't *shut up*," Breeze growled. "He was always going on and on and on about *you*. How brave you were and how kind you were and how you had *saved us all* by murdering our Alpha. Terror would never have stood for such disloyalty! Terror would have made him *eat his own tongue* . . . but anyway," she added, blinking, settling back into her calm, pleasant voice, "it was time. I needed to really get the Fear-Dog's attention, turn his gaze on your Pack. And it worked."

"And Bruno?" Storm growled through her teeth.

"Oh, Bruno had simply outlived his usefulness," said Breeze.

"He was so much help to me at first, he and Dart. They never liked you—the Fear-Dog walked with them from the start. He breathed in their ears and they spread my rumors faster than I ever could. And Bruno was so stupid, he never had any idea he was doing my will. I'm not sure what turned him, but when he came to me and said he thought we were wrong, that he was determined to clear your name . . . well, he had to go, before he did any more damage."

Storm's belly turned over and she thought she might bring up foul chunks. Bruno had died because he knew Storm was innocent, and Whisper because he just *liked* her too much.

This is all my fault, she thought.

"I should thank you, really," Breeze went on. "Leaving the Pack of your own accord was the best thing you could have done for me. Things were getting quite tense, but all I had to do was lie low for a while and not make any more trouble for them all to believe that you must have been the traitor all along. Now that I'm safe, the plan can move forward."

"Well I'm back now," Storm snarled. "And it's all over, Breeze. I'm going to tell the Pack everything. You'll want to be a long, long way away when Lucky hears how you tried to make his pups drown themselves."

Breeze barked a short laugh. "On the contrary, I'll be there to see that. *I'm* going to tell him, just before I rip his throat out."

Storm felt her hackles rising. Enough of this—it was time for Breeze to get what she deserved. Storm took a step forward, her teeth bared.

"I'm giving you a chance, Breeze. You don't deserve it, but because I'm not a savage dog, I'm going to give you one chance anyway. *Run*, far away, and perhaps I won't come after you."

"Oh, Storm, you silly dog," Breeze laughed, as if Storm had just slipped and fallen in the pond. "I'm not going anywhere! I'm not *finished*."

All right, then.

Storm tensed, a loud growl rumbling in her chest. "Yes," she said. "You are."

Breeze tilted her head, the laughter gone from her face, as Storm crouched to spring.

I'm glad she said no. I've had enough of bargaining. Let's do this—for Whisper and Bruno!

Her muscles bunched and released and she leaped a full dog-length across the clearing toward Breeze—

And then she skidded to a clumsy halt and stared in shock as Breeze put her head down and bit, hard, into her own shoulder.

She tore at herself and then shook her head at Storm, sending blood and fur spattering across Storm's face and neck. Storm cringed back. She should have expected something crazy from Breeze, but *this* ...

Breeze darted away from Storm and shot her a mad-eyed look of triumph before pinning her ears back and howling at the sky:

"Help! Lucky, it's the bad dog! She's trying to kill me!"

CHAPTER TWENTY-ONE

"*They won't save you, they're rabbit-chases* away," Storm snarled, scrambling to shake off the shock.

"*Are* they?" Breeze giggled. Storm advanced on her. She wouldn't let the bad dog win, she would break her neck before Lucky could get here.

Then she froze as she heard the unmistakable sound of something running through the forest, crunching the leaves and snapping the twigs.

"Breeze! Hold on!" Lucky howled.

You led me here. You knew they were nearby all along.

Storm just had time to throw Breeze a furious look before the hunting party crashed into the clearing. Lucky skidded to a halt between Breeze and Storm, his golden fur ruffled and his tongue out, panting from the sprint through the trees. He looked at Breeze, and the blood streaming from her shoulder and pooling under her paws. Then he looked at Storm, and his eyes went wide.

He said nothing, but simply stood and stared at her, a look in his eyes like he was seeing something completely impossible.

"Storm, no!" Mickey howled, and it was such a heartbroken sound that it made Storm want to sink down onto her belly and cover her eyes with her paws.

No, said a voice in her head, one that she knew was her own but came from somewhere deep down. *Don't give up. You can still tell them everything. Just stay calm!*

"She attacked me! It's—I can't believe it," Breeze howled mournfully. "It was her, after all this time! Storm's the traitor dog!"

"I am not," Storm managed to bark. But Snap still launched herself at her, and after a moment Mickey joined his mate. They barreled into her, and against every instinct she had, she let herself be knocked to the ground. "I'm not resisting!" she howled, trying to force herself to go limp while Snap jumped onto her back and clamped her jaws onto the scruff of her neck.

"You'd better not!" Snap growled through her mouthful of Storm's fur.

"Mickey, please, you know me," Storm whined. "It's not true!

I'm not the bad dog, it's *Breeze!*"

"*What?*" Mickey yapped. Storm's head was pressed to the ground and she couldn't move it to look, but she caught the ruffle of his fur as he looked up at Lucky.

"Oh, Storm, what has become of you?" Breeze said, and then paused, apparently trying to stifle a whimper of pain. "Why have you come back? Why did you do this to me? I don't understand."

It's her word against mine. But Lucky and Mickey will . . . I mean, they have to.

She looked up and saw Lucky staring down at her, his tail between his legs.

She remembered when she'd thought of him almost as a Father-Dog, when he and Mickey brought her out of the Dog-Garden, fought for her and her brothers to be accepted into the Pack, comforted them when they were afraid, taught them to survive . . . at least, they did their best.

They used to look at her with affection, with *pride*, and now all she saw in Lucky's eyes was fear and sadness.

"Lucky, you have to listen to me, she bit *herself* to make you *think* I'd attacked her!" Storm howled.

"There's blood on your face," whimpered Mickey.

"She put that there. She's the traitor! I came back to warn you all, I worked it out. It was Breeze all along."

"I don't understand," Breeze said again, and Storm saw her walk up to Lucky on trembling legs. "She came out of nowhere and she just attacked me. She was howling—all sorts of things, things that didn't make any sense."

Is she even really in pain, or faking it for them? Storm wondered.

Breeze leaned slightly against Lucky, putting her muzzle close to his neck. Storm twitched involuntarily and almost got to her paws, desperate to get up and take Breeze down before she could sink her teeth into Lucky, but Snap's teeth tightened on her scruff and she sank back with a despairing sigh.

"Don't believe her," she pleaded, through gritted teeth.

"Storm, it's *Breeze*," Lucky snapped. "What kind of motive would she have?"

"It's because of Terror," Storm began. "It's all to do with the Fear-Dog, and—"

Breeze cut her off. "Terror is *dead*, Storm. You saved us from him, don't you remember?" She looked at Lucky with dark eyes, full of pain and confusion. Storm's heart sank. If she hadn't known better, she wouldn't have believed Breeze was a killer either. "Do you think all of this has been some kind of . . . misplaced loyalty?" Breeze muttered. "Perhaps she even thought she was protecting us? Perhaps she thought that *Whisper* was the traitor. . . ."

"That's not true," said Storm flatly.

She laid her head down in the grass in a submissive gesture. She just didn't know what else to do.

They don't believe me, she thought. *No matter what I say about Breeze now, I'll just be confirming what she's said. They'll think I'm the one that's crazy.*

This was why she hadn't wanted to get the Pack involved. This, and the look of fear and heartbreak that still flickered over Lucky's and Mickey's faces.

"Why did you come back?" Mickey asked quietly. "You could have just stayed away."

Storm tried to ignore the gnawing sadness of his words. He didn't mean it—at least, he wouldn't if he knew the truth. She realized that Breeze had selected her target perfectly. This would never have worked with another dog. No matter what Breeze had done, no dog would ever mistrust Sunshine, or Daisy, or even Lucky in this way. The Pack had never been able to believe the best of Storm, even before Breeze arrived.

"What do we do with her?" Snap growled. "We can't let her go—what if she comes back and decides *you're* the bad dog, Lucky, or one of your *pups*?"

"What are you saying?" Lucky muttered. "We should keep her here? Living in the Pack with us?"

"We can't watch her day and night!" Snap growled.

Storm's fur rippled with fear as she realized what Snap was saying. She tried not to tense, because it would tip off the other dogs, but if she had to throw Snap off and run for her life, she would have to be ready. The little dog would get in a few hard bites on her neck, but Storm ought to be able to make it to the trees. . . .

Had it really come to this? A wave of intense loneliness washed over Storm. There was no dog here who would speak for her.

But I won't die here. Not like this.

Storm looked up at Breeze, but the bad dog was listening with a sad, bewildered tilt to her head. It was impossible to tell what she was really thinking.

"I don't want to kill her," said Snap, and Storm was surprised to feel a wave of choked emotion in her voice. "But I don't see what other option—"

"*No!*" Lucky barked. "No. We won't just kill her like a prey creature in the woods, all alone. Whatever she *may* have done, and we don't know for certain, she deserves better than that."

He shook himself. Storm felt like she should feel comforted by his words, but what use were they really? He still believed Breeze's story.

"Alpha is still the leader of this Pack. She's the only one who can make a decision like this. We'll bring Storm to her."

Storm's belly seemed to tighten uncomfortably. What would Sweet say about all this? She had loved Storm once, but not as much as Lucky, and if she thought Breeze was telling the truth . . .

"All right, Storm, I'm letting you go," said Snap, still through a mouthful of Storm's scruff. Lucky and Mickey walked up to her and stood close on either side, so when Snap let go and hopped off Storm's back, the two dogs were flanking her, too close for her to turn, close enough for one of them to sink their teeth in if she tried to attack the other. As close as they would have been the last time they shared the hunters' den together.

Snap took up the position in front of her, and Breeze slunk uneasily around behind her. Storm cast an angry look back, but Mickey growled, "Storm," and she faced front again.

"Get walking," said Lucky. "Just take it slowly and stay calm, all right, Storm? There are four of us. We'll be able to hunt you down if you run."

"I won't run," Storm said. She walked forward without hesitation. If only she knew how to convince them that she was more afraid of Breeze walking behind her tail, of that mad, twitching, snapping face she'd seen before they arrived, than she was of the other three combined.

They made slow, steady progress back toward the camp, mostly in silence. Storm didn't try to run, though she did briefly consider it when they came out into a wide, open field and she saw the Endless Lake gleaming on the horizon. But what would she do if she did escape them? Facing Sweet and the Pack was a terrible plan, but it was all Breeze had left her.

"Lucky," she said quietly, "please at least consider that I'm telling the truth. I'm not crazy. Just think about everything that's happened. Ask the pups about the rabbit blood in the camp again. Ask Tiny why she went to the lake."

Lucky shot her a puzzled, slightly angry look but didn't respond. Storm gave up trying to communicate with him. Perhaps he was too afraid to consider the truth, or he was still reeling from discovering that apparently, his adopted pup was a crazed killer after all. Either way, he was going to be no help to her now.

As they emerged from the trees and approached the bottom of the slope up to the Wild Pack camp, a high-pitched barking started up, and Storm saw four sandy-colored shapes bounding toward her from the pond. Tiny, Tumble, Nibble, and Fluff charged toward Storm, barking at the tops of their voices.

"Storm! You're back!" Tiny yipped. She was growing into her swift-dog heritage. Her small body balanced on long, thin legs that scrambled over the ground. Storm felt as if a thorn of ice was digging into her heart as she got her first really good look at the four litter-siblings.

Tumble was looking more and more like an elongated version of his Father-Dog, and Nibble and Fluff were so different she almost couldn't have said they were litter-sisters, Nibble with her very short tan fur and large, wary eyes, and Fluff with her long, darker fur blowing in the wind as she ran down the slope toward Storm.

"She's back!" Fluff echoed her litter-sister.

"Are you back to stay?" Tumble asked, a spark of hope in his voice that dug Storm's ice-thorn even deeper. He had forgiven her, then, for scaring him with their nighttime trip to the Endless Lake?

But before the pups could get to Storm, Lucky hurriedly put himself between them, keeping them at a distance.

"Breeze, get Sunshine to help you clean your wound," he barked. Breeze slunk around Storm, limping with her tail between her legs, drawing the pups' attention.

"What happened?" Nibble whined. "Are you all right? Breeze?"

"I'm all right now, pups," said Breeze. "Let's go and see Sunshine."

"But Storm . . ." Tiny frowned.

"Come away from her," Breeze yapped hurriedly, her tail clamped low.

She's pretending to be afraid of me, Storm thought. She tried to stay still, and not to growl at Breeze no matter how deep and dark her hatred ran, but she didn't know if there was much point. The pups did as they were told, though Tiny kept glancing back at Storm, her little tail lashing with worry.

Mickey and Snap nudged Storm, and she followed the pups and Breeze up the slope to the middle of the Pack camp, walking slowly. By the time she got there, Breeze must have already started to spread her lies through her Packmates, because the dogs were gathering, staring at Storm in horror as she padded into their camp. Daisy, Chase, Moon, Thorn, and Beetle all stood around the clearing between the fallen tree and the dens, their tails between their legs and their ears pricked with shock or flat with worry. Daisy was clawing the ground anxiously with one little black paw, and Thorn and Beetle were whispering urgently to each other.

And there was Sunshine, fussing at Breeze's wound. She looked up at Storm and her small, gleaming black eyes grew wider than Storm had ever seen them before. She was trembling, making the thin white hairs that covered her whole body ripple like the surface of the Endless Lake.

They really think I'm the bad dog, Storm thought. *Breeze probably thinks she's won.*

Storm glanced at Breeze, and then looked up as there was a rustle from the den and Sweet stepped out, wary confusion in her large swift-dog eyes.

"What's going on here?" she demanded.

At once, the camp dissolved into chaos.

CHAPTER TWENTY-TWO

"It's Storm!"

"Breeze is hurt!"

"She's the bad dog!"

"Mother-Dog . . ."

"We're in danger, Alpha!"

"Quiet!" Sweet howled.

Storm stood at the edge of the camp, still under guard. Thorn had joined Mickey and Snap, keeping Storm cornered with her back to an impenetrable tangle of twigs. Thorn wouldn't meet her eyes.

"Beta, what is going on?" Sweet barked. "And the rest of you, *quiet!*" she added, as Moon and Snap both opened their jaws to respond.

Lucky padded up to Sweet, looking as if he was carrying heavy rocks tied to his fur.

SURVIVORS: THE GATHERING DARKNESS

"We found Storm in the woods near the weasel dens. Apparently, she came out of nowhere and attacked Breeze."

"She did!" Breeze panted. "I couldn't believe it. Storm, I thought we were friends! I never thought you were the bad dog. But now . . ." She trailed off, shaking her head, a vision of sadness and betrayal.

I'm going to kill you, Storm thought, a cold certainty settling in her belly. She tried not to let the hate show on her face. *For Whisper and Bruno. I can't believe I ever thought we were friends.*

"Breeze bit herself," she said, barking loud and clear so that every dog in the camp heard it. "I only came back because I realized that Breeze is the bad dog."

"She's mad," Breeze whined, lying down and putting her paws over her muzzle. "Oh, Spirit Dogs, how could you have let Storm go so wrong?"

"Breeze, be quiet for a minute, please," said Sweet, and Storm's ears pricked up despite herself. Could it be? Did Sweet believe her, after all? Had Breeze gone too far with her shocked-and-heartbroken act? "Storm, you were once part of this Pack, and I used to believe you could be trusted—just as I trust Breeze. Therefore, I *will* give you a chance to explain yourself, and then Breeze will have a chance to speak. Do you accept that this is fair?"

Storm suddenly had a vivid memory of sitting at the top of the wolf valley, peering over the edge at the wolves surrounding Peaceful. This was her only chance to explain herself, and she had to stay calm and seize the moment. There was no Great Wolf here compelling her to tell the truth, but she knew Breeze would lie to the face of the Spirit Dogs if she could—the only one she cared about was the Fear-Dog, and he probably lined his den with lies.

"Yes, Sweet," she said, dipping her head submissively.

"Then explain."

Storm's jaws suddenly felt dry, and she licked her lips nervously. The Pack was watching her. Daisy was sitting with the pups, who were huddled close together, their eyes wide. Beetle's hackles were raised, and Moon seemed as if she was in such shock she could hardly react at all. Beside her, Mickey's sides rose and fell as he took and released a very deep breath.

"I trusted Breeze too," she said. "Until I left the Pack, and I started to put the clues together. Breeze has been trying to get revenge for Terror's death. She's been going after every dog who was there when it happened. She targeted me, made you all suspect me, and made me leave the Pack, because I killed him. She's the one who told the pups stories about the lake—hoping that they'd wander into it and drown—to attack Lucky. She framed

Moon for stealing food and tried to crush her in a rock trap. She poisoned Bella's prey and put clear-stone in Twitch's. She killed Whisper because he was so happy that Terror was gone. She confessed everything to me—how she wanted to bring the Fear-Dog here and tear the Pack apart. She murdered Bruno because he wanted to clear my name."

The Pack dogs were looking at one another, and Storm saw disbelief as well as a few shivers of fear. She couldn't tell if any of them believed her.

"I spoke to Rake and the others, and they said she was the only dog in Terror's Pack who was truly loyal to him, and not just afraid of him. And Arrow said he saw her bringing a live, bleeding rabbit back to the camp, prolonging its suffering," she said. "She was the one who smeared that blood all around the camp."

Lucky's ears pricked up. "You saw Arrow? Was Bella with him?"

Storm stared at him. She couldn't believe that in all of this, she hadn't told him about his litter-sister. "Yes . . . they're my Pack now. They're living in a forest near the High Ground. Bella has two pups, both males. They're doing really well."

Lucky's tongue lolled from his mouth happily, and then he

seemed to remember what was happening and his expression settled back into worry.

"Is that everything you have to say, Storm?" Sweet prompted.

"Breeze admitted it all," Storm said. "I confronted her, and she told me exactly what she was doing and why. Then she bit herself on the shoulder and howled for help. That's when Lucky arrived."

"This is all ridiculous," muttered Moon, though she looked at Breeze and a shudder ran through her fur.

"I know," Storm said. "But it's true. And she's not finished. You're all in terrible danger if you let her go free."

"Breeze?" Sweet asked, turning to the bad dog. Storm was exhausted and disgusted to see that Breeze was trembling, and a low, frightened whine came from her throat.

"Storm, you have to stop this," she said. "If you stop making these things up now, perhaps Alpha will let you live. You could even go back to Bella. Although . . . her pups . . ."

"I could have fought you all off," Storm put in. "I could have run away, but instead I let Lucky and Mickey and Snap bring me here, so that I could explain it all to you. I just want to protect this Pack."

"You've had your chance, Storm," Sweet snapped. "Let Breeze speak."

"I don't . . . I don't have anything to say!" Breeze muttered, as if she was trying *so hard* to work out Storm's actions that it was hurting her head. "I don't know why Storm would choose *me* to blame, but then, why Whisper? Why Bruno? I think she's telling the truth that she wants to protect us. Especially your pups. But if her idea of protection is *murder* . . . who's to say she won't hurt them too, if we just let her go?"

You!

Storm stifled a howl of rage by dipping her head again, the closest she'd come to letting her emotions overtake her. But a frothing, violent Fierce Dog was what Breeze was suggesting she had become, and she would not give her the satisfaction of playing it out for the Pack to see.

"Storm would never hurt us," said a small voice, and Storm raised her head to see Tiny stepping forward in front of her Mother-Dog, her ears pricked up with determination. "I don't think she's the bad dog, and I don't think she'd lie, either." The pup didn't look at Breeze, even though she must know what believing Storm would mean.

Storm's heart swelled in her chest, with love and with anxiety about what Breeze might do now. *Tiny, thank you, but please be careful!* She might have been a runt once, but she was as brave as any grown dog.

"Shush, Tiny," said Sweet. "You're only a pup, you don't know what you're saying."

Storm winced as she saw an expression of hurt and anger pass across Tiny's face. It was painfully familiar. The pup stepped aside and sat down next to Daisy, her brows drawn down and her tail lashing in agitation.

So Sweet and Lucky won't listen to their own pups either.

It was almost reassuring, to know that they believed they were right even when the pup telling them otherwise *wasn't* a half-grown Fierce Dog. She wished she could tell Tiny all the times the Pack would have been better off if they'd listened to her.

"It can't be Breeze," Chase spoke up. "What Rake said about how she was in Terror's Pack is true, but we all had to find our own ways to cope. It doesn't mean anything. She's a gentle dog! Whereas Storm . . ."

She left that hanging in the air, and Storm sat down.

This again. "Storm is . . . well . . . we wouldn't want to be mean, we're sure it's not just *that she's a Fierce Dog*, but, well, you know . . ."

She didn't even know if dogs like Chase truly believed that

Fierce Dogs were uncontrollably violent; it was just something they'd been told so often they didn't think before they repeated it.

"So what do we do?" Daisy asked, her voice shaking.

"If Storm's dangerous," Chase said, "then we can't let her go, and we can't keep her here. We don't want the bad dog back here, do we?"

All the dogs shook their heads.

"The pups are growing fast, but they're still vulnerable," said Snap slowly. "How far would we need to drive her out, before we felt safe? I hate this as much as any of you, but if Storm lives, we may never sleep soundly in our dens again."

"What?" Daisy yipped, almost falling over in her rush to get to her paws. "Kill Storm? Are you crazy? We're not doing that!"

"But if she's telling the truth about Bella and her pups, how do we know *they'd* be safe?" said Chase. Lucky twitched at this, and he looked at Storm and then at Breeze. "If she's crazy, we can't just let her wander off to torment another Pack!"

"I'm not crazy, and I would never hurt Nip or Scramble," Storm said, as evenly as she could manage.

"Storm's a good dog. She's saved all our lives at some point or other," Twitch pointed out slowly. "Even when some of us weren't all that keen on her being in our Pack."

Sweet cocked her head at this, as if what the Third Dog had said had made her think of something, but she didn't interrupt.

"I don't care if she is mad," Daisy yipped. "I won't let you hurt her, she's . . . she's our responsibility, even if she has lost her mind!"

"Daisy's right," said Breeze, and all the dogs turned to look at her. "I don't mind that she's accusing me. She shouldn't be killed for that. Maybe it's all Blade's fault—look at how she was treated, losing her litter-brothers the way she did, being trapped in that Dog-Garden with her Mother-Dog's body for days . . . it all must have taken a far greater toll than we thought."

Storm's hackles rose. *How dare you talk about my Mother-Dog or my litter-brothers.*

"So how do you propose we control her?" Chase barked. "She's twice as big as some of us!"

"I don't know," Breeze said miserably. "Perhaps she could be . . . wounded. To make her harmless. Perhaps . . . if she was blind . . ."

Storm felt as if a freezing wave from the Endless Lake had just washed over her. Breeze met her eyes, and just for a second Storm thought she could see something black and enormous looking back.

"No!" Mickey howled. "Alpha, that would be so *cruel.*"

"Dogs can live good lives when they're blind," said Chase slowly. "I knew an old dog once who—"

"This isn't the same! You're talking about *intentionally blinding her*," Twitch cried. "A dog can live with a lot, but that kind of betrayal—"

"She betrayed us first!" snapped Chase.

"All right," said Sweet, in a quiet voice that nonetheless seemed to shut down the barking all around her. "That's enough. I've heard everything I need to hear. And I'm not making the decision to kill or maim a dog right this moment. All of this needs more consideration. For tonight, Storm will remain here as our captive. We'll put her in my own den, with three dogs on guard at all times to make sure she doesn't dig her way out. Lucky, the pups, and I will sleep in the hunters' and Patrol Dogs' dens tonight."

There was a short pause, and then Sweet turned her stare on Chase, and Chase sat down on her haunches and dipped her head. "Yes, Alpha."

A chorus of "Yes, Alphas" ran around the camp, and Sweet turned her gaze on Storm.

"I expect you to cooperate," she said. "If you don't, I'll have no choice but to take Breeze's advice and make sure you can't escape justice. Is that understood?"

Storm sagged to the ground, all the energy draining from her. "Yes, Alpha," she said.

Mickey nudged Storm again, and she turned and headed for the Alpha's den.

I never imagined I might sleep here, she thought, as she ducked her head to go in through the dark entrance, *and especially not as a prisoner.*

When she was inside, she turned and looked out and saw the four pups standing nearby, misery and confusion in the thumping of their tails and the drooping of their ears. She wanted to say something, but a thick tangle of twigs was dragged across the entrance, blocking them from view.

What would she have said, anyway? *It's going to be all right?*

She wasn't sure it was.

Alpha's den was large, warm, and comfortable, partly dug down into the earth, lined with the freshest moss. Above her the twisting branches of a large bush with tiny, bright red-brown leaves formed a complete dome, sheltering Alpha and her family from the wind and rain, and coincidentally giving Storm no chance to escape.

Storm turned an angry sleep-circle, stomping down the moss under her paws, then settled down in the center of the den. The scents of Sweet, Lucky, and the four pups were so strong and so relaxed that she let out a sad whine.

I knew this would happen. Or something like this. I knew if I came back to the Wild Pack, they would believe Breeze and not me.

That they would consider blinding or killing her . . . that she hadn't expected. But that was Breeze, suggesting things, wriggling her opinions in wherever she could, fooling all the other dogs with her trembling and her whining.

They're being driven by the Fear-Dog. I can smell *him. How can I convince dogs who are so afraid they'd turn on their own Packmates?*

I can't. So what good am I?

Outside the den, she smelled dogs close by—probably her guards—and heard the mutter and bark of the Pack attempting to go on with their normal Pack tasks. There was a fearful whining note to all the dogs' voices, and Storm could tell that they were all in for a restless night.

But the danger isn't in here—it's out there with you, eating your prey, watching your pups, putting ideas into your heads.

Storm sighed and laid her head on the moss, closing her eyes.

She'd felt less alone when she was running through the forests, starving and drenched from the river, than she did now that she was surrounded by dogs who said they were her friends but wouldn't believe her when she told them they were in danger.

I have to save the pups . . . I have to save them all, even if they think I'm crazy.

But what could she do from inside her prison?

Spirit Dogs, you've helped me before. You saved me from the river. You took me to Thoughtful and Peaceful. You kept Bella and two of her pups alive.

Help me now. Earth-Dog, River-Dog, Watch-Dog . . . help me save my Pack.

There was no response from the Spirit Dogs. The light that filtered into the den through the branches grew weaker and weaker, and soon Storm was almost lying in the dark. She heard more barking outside, the soft rustle of many dogs walking over Red Leaf grass and gathering together. It must be time for their meal. Storm's stomach rumbled.

Then the tangle of twigs moved, and the last light of the Sun-Dog spilled into the den. Storm's heart gave a lurch of gratefulness and worry as she saw Sunshine squeeze inside with a rabbit leg clutched in her tiny jaws.

"Thank you," Storm whined. "Sunshine, I—"

"Shh," said the tiny white dog. She dropped the rabbit, and then she walked right up to Storm's muzzle and licked her nose. "I believe you," she whispered. "And I'm not the only one."

"Sunshine?" said Chase's voice from outside in an anxious

whine. "Are you all right? Do you need me to come in there?"

"I'm fine," Sunshine barked back. She turned her beady black eyes on Storm, and hope blossomed painfully in Storm's chest. She nuzzled the little dog, almost knocking her over. Sunshine gave her another brief lick on the side of her face, and then she was gone, scrambling up and out of the den. The twigs were pushed back across the entrance and the light went out.

Storm lay in the darkness, her heart pounding. Sunshine was so little, and she was the Pack's Omega. It wasn't much of a hope. There was little she could do, if Breeze decided to strike while Storm was still being held captive.

But it was still hope. The Fear-Dog might be stalking them, but Storm knew she could face him, as long as she didn't have to do it all alone.

As long as Sunshine believed in her, the Fear-Dog would never win.

She wouldn't let it.

ERIN HUNTER

is inspired by a fascination with the ferocity of the natural world. As well as having great respect for nature in all its forms, Erin enjoys creating rich, mythical explanations for animal behavior. She is also the author of the Survivors, Seekers, and Bravelands series.

Download the free Warriors app at www.warriorcats.com.

HEED THE CALL OF THE WILD . . .

A NEW ERIN HUNTER ADVENTURE BEGINS

BRAVELANDS

For generations, the animals of the African plains have been ruled by the code of the wild: only kill to survive. But when an unthinkable act of betrayal shatters the peace, a young lion, a baboon, and an elephant calf will be thrust together in an epic battle for survival. The fragile balance between predators and prey now rests in the paws of these three unlikely heroes. . . .

CHAPTER 1

Swiftcub pounced after the vulture's shadow, but it flitted away too quickly to follow. Breathing hard, he pranced back to his pride. *I saw that bird off our territory,* he thought, delighted. *No rot-eater's going to come near Gallantpride while I'm around!*

The pride needed him to defend it, Swiftcub thought, picking up his paws and strutting around his family. Why, right now they were all half asleep, dozing and basking in the shade of the acacia trees. The most energetic thing the other lions were doing was lifting their heads to groom their nearest neighbors, or their own paws. They had no *idea* of the threat Swiftcub had just banished.

I might be only a few moons old, but my father is the strongest, bravest lion in Bravelands. And I'm going to be just like him!

"Swiftcub!"

The gentle but commanding voice snapped him out of his

dreams of glory. He came to a halt, turning and flicking his ears at the regal lioness who stood over him.

"Mother," he said, shifting on his paws.

"Why are you shouting at vultures?" Swift scolded him fondly, licking at his ears. "They're nothing but scavengers. Come on, you and your sister can play later. Right now you're supposed to be practicing hunting. And if you're going to catch anything, you'll need to keep your eyes on the prey, not on the sky!"

"Sorry, Mother." Guiltily he padded after her as she led him through the dry grass, her tail swishing. The ground rose gently, and Swiftcub had to trot to keep up. The grasses tickled his nose, and he was so focused on trying not to sneeze, he almost bumped into his mother's haunches as she crouched.

"Oops," he growled.

Valor shot him a glare. His older sister was hunched a little to the left of their mother, fully focused on their hunting practice. Valor's sleek body was low to the ground, her muscles tense; as she moved one paw forward with the utmost caution, Swiftcub tried to copy her, though it was hard to keep up on his much shorter legs. One creeping pace, then two. Then another.

I'm being very quiet, just like Valor. I'm going to be a great hunter. He slunk up alongside his mother, who remained quite still.

"There, Swiftcub," she murmured. "Do you see the burrows?"

He did, now. Ahead of the three lions, the ground rose up even higher, into a bare, sandy mound dotted with small shadowy holes. As Swiftcub watched, a small nose and whiskers poked out, testing the air. The meerkat emerged completely, stood up on its hind legs, and stared around. Satisfied, it stuck out a pink tongue and began to groom its chest, as more meerkats appeared beyond it. Growing in confidence, they scurried farther away from their burrows.

"Careful now," rumbled Swift. "They're very quick. Go!"

Swiftcub sprang forward, his little paws bounding over the ground. Still, he wasn't fast enough to outpace Valor, who was far ahead of him already. A stab of disappointment spoiled his excitement, and suddenly it was even harder to run fast, but he ran grimly after his sister.

The startled meerkats were already doubling back into their holes. Stubby tails flicked and vanished; the bigger leader, his round dark eyes glaring at the oncoming lions, was last to twist and dash underground. Valor's jaws snapped at his tail, just missing.

"Sky and stone!" the bigger cub swore, coming to a halt in a cloud of dust. She shook her head furiously and licked her jaws. "I nearly had it!"

A rumble of laughter made Swiftcub turn. His father, Gallant, stood watching them. Swiftcub couldn't help but feel the usual twinge of awe mixed in with his delight. Black-maned and huge, his sleek fur glowing golden in the sun, Gallant would have been intimidating if Swiftcub hadn't known and loved him so well. Swift rose to her paws and greeted the great lion affectionately, rubbing his maned neck with her head.

"It was a good attempt, Valor," Gallant reassured his

daughter. "What Swift said is true: meerkats are *very* hard to catch. You were so close—one day you'll be as fine a hunter as your mother." He nuzzled Swift and licked her neck.

"*I* wasn't anywhere near it," grumbled Swiftcub. "I'll never be as fast as Valor."

"Oh, you will," said Gallant. "Don't forget, Valor's a whole year older than you, my son. You're getting bigger and faster every day. Be patient!" He stepped closer, leaning in so his great tawny muzzle brushed Swiftcub's own. "That's the secret to stalking, too. Learn patience, and one day you will be a *very* fine hunter."

"I hope so," said Swiftcub meekly.

Gallant nuzzled him. "Don't doubt yourself, my cub. You're going to be a great lion and the best kind of leader: one who keeps his own pride safe and content, but puts fear into the heart of his strongest enemy!"

That does sound good! Feeling much better, Swiftcub nodded. Gallant nipped affectionately at the tufty fur on top of his head and padded toward Valor.

Swiftcub watched him proudly. *He's right, of course. Father knows everything! And I will be a great hunter, I will. And a brave, strong leader—*

A tiny movement caught his eye, a scuttling shadow in his father's path.

A scorpion!

Barely pausing to think, Swiftcub sprang, bowling between his father's paws and almost tripping him. He skidded to a halt right in front of Gallant, snarling at the small sand-yellow scorpion. It paused, curling up its barbed tail and raising its pincers in threat.

"No, Swiftcub!" cried his father.

Swiftcub swiped his paw sideways at the creature, catching its plated shell and sending it flying into the long grass.

All four lions watched the grass, holding their breath, waiting for a furious scorpion to reemerge. But there was no stir of movement. It must have fled. Swiftcub sat back, his heart suddenly banging against his ribs.

"Skies above!" Gallant laughed. Valor gaped, and Swift dragged her cub into her paws and began to lick him roughly.

"Mother . . ." he protested.

"Honestly, Swiftcub!" she scolded him as her tongue swept across his face. "Your father might have gotten a nasty sting from that creature—but *you* could have been killed!"

"You're such an idiot, little brother," sighed Valor, but there was admiration in her eyes.

Gallant and Swift exchanged proud looks. "Swift," growled Gallant, "I do believe the time has come to give our cub his true name."

Swift nodded, her eyes shining. "Now that we know what kind of lion he is, I think you're right."

Gallant turned toward the acacia trees, his tail lashing, and gave a resounding roar.

It always amazed Swiftcub that the pride could be lying half asleep one moment and alert the very next. Almost before Gallant had finished roaring his summons, there was a rustle of grass, a crunch of paws on dry earth, and the rest of Gallantpride appeared, ears pricked and eyes bright with curiosity. Gallant huffed in greeting, and the twenty lionesses and young lions of his pride spread out in a circle around him, watching and listening intently.

Gallant looked down again at Swiftcub, who blinked and glanced away, suddenly rather shy. "Crouch down," murmured the great lion.

When he obeyed, Swiftcub felt his father's huge paw rest on his head.

"Henceforth," declared Gallant, "this cub of mine will no longer be known as Swiftcub. He faced a dangerous foe without hesitation and protected his pride. His name, now and forever, is Fearless Gallantpride."

It was done so quickly, Swiftcub felt dizzy with astonishment. *I have my name! I'm Fearless. Fearless Gallantpride!*

All around him, his whole family echoed his name, roaring their approval. Their deep cries resonated across the grasslands.

"Fearless Gallantpride!"

"Welcome, Fearless, son of Gallant!"

His heart swelled inside him. Suddenly, he knew what it was to be a full member of the pride. He had to half close his eyes and flatten his ears, he felt so buffeted by their roars of approval.

"I'll—I promise I'll live up to my name!" he managed to growl. It came out a little squeakier than he'd intended, but no lion laughed at him. They bellowed their delight even more.

"Of course you will," murmured Swift.

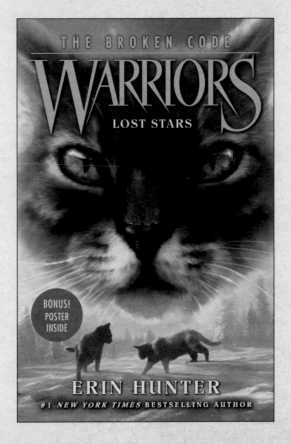

WARRIORS

How many have you read?

Dawn of the Clans
- ○ #1: The Sun Trail
- ○ #2: Thunder Rising
- ○ #3: The First Battle
- ○ #4: The Blazing Star
- ○ #5: A Forest Divided
- ○ #6: Path of Stars

Power of Three
- ○ #1: The Sight
- ○ #2: Dark River
- ○ #3: Outcast
- ○ #4: Eclipse
- ○ #5: Long Shadows
- ○ #6: Sunrise

The Prophecies Begin
- ○ #1: Into the Wild
- ○ #2: Fire and Ice
- ○ #3: Forest of Secrets
- ○ #4: Rising Storm
- ○ #5: A Dangerous Path
- ○ #6: The Darkest Hour

Omen of the Stars
- ○ #1: The Fourth Apprentice
- ○ #2: Fading Echoes
- ○ #3: Night Whispers
- ○ #4: Sign of the Moon
- ○ #5: The Forgotten Warrior
- ○ #6: The Last Hope

The New Prophecy
- ○ #1: Midnight
- ○ #2: Moonrise
- ○ #3: Dawn
- ○ #4: Starlight
- ○ #5: Twilight
- ○ #6: Sunset

A Vision of Shadows
- ○ #1: The Apprentice's Quest
- ○ #2: Thunder and Shadow
- ○ #3: Shattered Sky
- ○ #4: Darkest Night
- ○ #5: River of Fire
- ○ #6: The Raging Storm

Select titles also available as audiobooks!

HARPER

An Imprint of HarperCollinsPublishers

www.warriorcats.com • www.shelfstuff.com

SUPER EDITIONS

- ◯ Firestar's Quest
- ◯ Bluestar's Prophecy
- ◯ SkyClan's Destiny
- ◯ Crookedstar's Promise
- ◯ Yellowfang's Secret
- ◯ Tallstar's Revenge
- ◯ Bramblestar's Storm
- ◯ Moth Flight's Vision
- ◯ Hawkwing's Journey
- ◯ Tigerheart's Shadow
- ◯ Crowfeather's Trial

GUIDES

- ◯ Secrets of the Clans
- ◯ Cats of the Clans
- ◯ Code of the Clans
- ◯ Battles of the Clans
- ◯ Enter the Clans
- ◯ The Ultimate Guide

FULL-COLOR MANGA

- ◯ Graystripe's Adventure
- ◯ Ravenpaw's Path
- ◯ SkyClan and the Stranger

Coming soon!

EBOOKS AND NOVELLAS

The Untold Stories
- ◯ Hollyleaf's Story
- ◯ Mistystar's Omen
- ◯ Cloudstar's Journey

Tales from the Clans
- ◯ Tigerclaw's Fury
- ◯ Leafpool's Wish
- ◯ Dovewing's Silence

Shadows of the Clans
- ◯ Mapleshade's Vengeance
- ◯ Goosefeather's Curse
- ◯ Ravenpaw's Farewell

Legends of the Clans
- ◯ Spottedleaf's Heart
- ◯ Pinestar's Choice
- ◯ Thunderstar's Echo